the Wish List 4

Survival of the Sparkliest!

the Wish List

the Wish List 4

Survival of the Sparkliest!

By Sarah Aronson

Scholastic Press
New York

Library of Congress Cataloging-in-Publication Data available

ISBN 978-0-545-94165-5

10 9 8 7 6 5 4 3 2 1   19 20 21 22 23

Printed in the U.S.A. 23

First edition, February 2019

Book design by Maeve Norton

For all my friends at the
Highlights Foundation

Chapter One

Exclamation Points and Capital Letters

Dear Trainees,

We are SO VERY HAPPY to welcome you to your final level of fairy godmother training. Thank you for everything you accomplished!!! We CAN'T WAIT to see what you do next!!! We believe in you!

—the Bests

Isabelle had never seen so many exclamation points or capital letters in one note.

Never before had the Bests thanked her for anything.

Never before had the Bests been excited to see what she could do.

Never before had the Bests ever even hinted they believed in her.

But today they did all three.

Before she could consider all the fairy godmother rules about early declarations of victory (or, in other words, over-confidence), Isabelle leaped on top of her bed and started dancing. She felt like a princess whose wishes had all just come true. The Bests liked her! They really liked her!

Becoming an official fairy godmother was in the bag!

For extra luck, Isabelle slipped on the bracelet that Nora, her friend and first practice princess, made for her when Isabelle (illegally) visited her summer camp. Then she got the shiny ring she'd found dangling on the girlgoyle's toe at the end of Level Two. Isabelle was 99.9 percent sure the ring had once belonged to Mom. Because Nora had a simi-lar (non-magical) ring, she also believed that the ring meant something important.

But so far, she couldn't figure out what that was.

Her sister (and the fourth-best fairy godmother), Clotilda, didn't think she should waste her time thinking about trinkets and other non-magical coincidences. She told Isabelle (too many times), "There are no shortcuts to becoming a great fairy godmother. If you want to pass Level Four, you have to be prepared." In other words: Learn all the rules.

This was the problem with having an older, smarter sister who knew everything. It was also the problem with not studying. And skipping the fine print. And it was the problem with daydreaming when she should have been paying attention. Isabelle was really disorganized. Even on this most important morning, she couldn't remember where she left her books. Or her glasses. Or, for that matter, her wand.

She didn't need Clotilda to tell her she'd better find them fast.

First, Isabelle checked the obvious places, like her nightstand, under the covers, and the floor near her bed. Then she tried less obvious spots, like behind the headboard and in the laundry basket. And when she still hadn't found them, she looked in the places they would never be, like next to the toilet and in her underwear drawer.

In the fairy godmother world, just as in the regular one, it is hard to find lost things when you can't see clearly. But it is easy to find things you aren't looking for.

In this case, Isabelle stumbled on a couple of cookies from her last sleepover with her fellow trainees, Angelica and Fawn, as well as a crumpled-up copy of W.A.R., the manifesto written by the Worsts (officially now the Grands) that had led to the strike in Level Three. She almost tripped over a whole bouquet of balloons, mostly still inflated, from last night's Extravaganza/birthday party, which were sitting on top of a large stack of . . . there they were! Her books! And her glasses, too.

When she put them on, she found another surprise sticking out of the top book on the pile. It was a bookmark that looked like a magic wand. Written on the bookmark was a note from her sister. (She knew it was from Clotilda because the handwriting was full of fancy curlicues and *i*'s dotted with stars.)

It said:

If you want to have an easy peasy first day of Level Four (just as I did), please memorize the marked section. Do it right now. Then meet me downstairs. Love, Clotilda.

Underneath was a PS: *You can thank me later.*

And in very tiny letters underneath that, a PPS: *If you pulled the bookmark out without marking the page, please turn to* The Official Guide to the Spectrum of Sparkles.

(Clotilda knew her sister well!)

Luckily, *The Official Guide to the Spectrum of Sparkles* was a gigantic pullout guide in the centerfold of the rule book—so it was easy to find. It displayed in great detail every single sparkle shade, as well as a handy key to explain the magical properties of each and every color.

There were tons of them.

Colors like Razzmatazz (a shade of red pink that produces giggles), Plum Passion (a color that helps princesses compromise), and one she couldn't even pronounce! It was a part-yellow and part-green shade called chartreuse, and according to the key, it helps princesses anticipate trouble.

She was just thinking how great it would be to have a chartreuse sparkle for herself when Grandmomma appeared at the door. She was still wearing her robe and slippers. In her hand was Isabelle's wand.

Grandmomma did not look happy.

Isabelle dashed to the door. "Good morning, Grandmomma. What a sparkly surprise! Thank you for bringing me my wand. How careless of me to misplace it."

This might seem overly formal, but Grandmomma (with the emphasis on *grand*) was the president of the Fairy Godmother Alliance; the editor of *The Official Rule Book for Fairy Godmothers*, now in its twelfth edition; and usually in the middle of some very important fairy godmother business, so she didn't enjoy returning lost wands (especially when the careless fairy godmother was one of her granddaughters).

Thankfully, she didn't stay annoyed for long. "Did you have a fine evening last night?" she asked. "Did you learn anything new?" Before Isabelle could answer,

Grandmomma patted her shoulder. "Are you ready to return to training and become an official fairy godmother?"

Isabelle knew just how to answer *that* question. "Not just ready, but I'm feeling it!" She demonstrated her newest signature style: a flick of the wrist and an extra-large swooping figure eight with a bit of a kick for gusto. Then she tripped over her books, fell down, and sent those balloons flying.

When the balloons hit the ceiling, Grandmomma took out her wand. "Would you mind if we straightened up a bit?"

Of course, Isabelle didn't mind. Fairy godmothers almost never used their sparkles for mundane tasks like cleaning.

Even more exciting (and rare), Grandmomma invited Isabelle to put her own hands on top of hers. Then, together, with one long sweeping motion and a couple of flicks and jabs, loose papers zoomed around the room like paper airplanes. The blankets on Isabelle's bed aired themselves out and tucked themselves tightly into the corners. The whole room smelled of roses. Or maybe lilacs. Isabelle didn't know the difference. Lickety-split, the rest of Isabelle's books made their way to the desk.

Isabelle's hands tingled. "That was amazing!"

Grandmomma flicked her wand one last time. "My dear, don't let anyone tell you otherwise. You were born to sparkle."

A shiny gold paper appeared out of nowhere and floated to Isabelle's now-clean desk. Isabelle smiled. "For me?"

She hoped it was a magical gift (something to help her out in training), but it wasn't. It was a practice quiz. On pretty paper.

"Make an old godmother happy and show me how ready you really are," Grandmomma said.

Isabelle tried to concentrate and fill in all the blanks, but it was hard with a powerful godmother looking over her shoulder and staring at her.

Still, she wanted to make Grandmomma proud, so she wrote down all the colors she could remember, including red for girl power, blue for loyalty, and yellow for fear, as well as:

Green: leadership
Orange: confidence
Purple: trust
Light blue: friendship

Grandmomma's hands quivered with enthusiasm. "Read through the spectrum one more time, then come to the kitchen. Your sister's been up since dawn creating an extra-special good-luck breakfast. You definitely don't want it to get cold."

Normally, Isabelle wouldn't have hesitated. (Clotilda never made breakfast for Isabelle.) But then she remembered the girlgoyles and decided to check on them first. Last night, she had given them each a shriveled blue sparkle (the ones that had been stored in her ring), so she grabbed her book and slippers and climbed to the top of the tower to the cozy spot to see whether anything magical had occurred overnight.

To her disappointment, the girlgoyles' hands were empty. More disappointing, nothing seemed different. The girlgoyles looked the way they always looked—friendly statues made of rock.

Isabelle did not know that last night those sparkles *had* worked—if only for a few moments.

The girlgoyles had come to life. Their names were Francoise and Bernadette, and they were French and sort of funny. They chatted and high-fived and tried very hard to get her attention with fireworks. This was because they had to tell her something—and obviously, it was something that was really important.

Unfortunately, since Isabelle had been extremely tired, she went to bed before they could tell her anything.

She didn't get the hint when they made fireworks in the sky.

This might sound sad, but because she didn't know what they said or what she missed, she didn't feel mad at herself at all. Instead, she did what she always did when she sat between her friends. She admired the green grass, the blue sky, and the shining sun that got energy from every single color in the spectrum of sparkles. Then she listened for birds and also frogs and mice, too. She also thought about Nora, and what she might wish for.

And then she did something new: She opened her book and read through the entire spectrum, four complete times.

Last, she thought about Mom. Wherever she was. She still hoped that someday she would see her. And that when that happened, Mom would be proud of her.

More than ever, Isabelle wished she could make everything right between Mom and the fairy godmother world. (No matter what everyone else said, she did not believe that her mother was the worst fairy godmother ever.) Maybe now that Isabelle was in Level Four, she would finally find out what had really happened. And why.

When she stood up, Isabelle could feel strong magic in the air (or at least, she thought that's what that breeze meant). Even though confidence alone wasn't a good thing, she had it! And she could feel it growing.

This was it!

Her final level of training.

No one could ruin her mood now!

Chapter Two

French Toast with a Side Order of Bad News

No one, maybe, except Clotilda.

When Isabelle slid down the shiny banister toward the kitchen, her sister waited for her at the bottom in a glittery blue apron. Her wand was neatly tucked into her topknot bun.

"Thanks for your note," Isabelle told her sister. "But you don't have to worry. I'm more than ready for Level Four."

"I don't want to scare you, but Level Four is challenging," Clotilda said, looking more than a little bit skeptical. "It isn't called Survival of the Sparkliest for nothing."

"'Survival of the Sparkliest'?" Isabelle's stomach did backflips. "You're joking, right?"

When Clotilda insisted she never joked (this was true), Isabelle reached into her pocket for the note from the Bests, the one with all those exclamation points. "They didn't say anything about survival." Even though it wasn't nice to brag, she added, "Read the whole thing. They said they believed in me."

Clotilda rolled her eyes. "We sent that note to everyone."

That was a disappointment. But that didn't make it untrue. So even though Isabelle was less hungry than she had been before talking to her sister, she piled her plate high with French toast with ribbons of chocolate, perfectly cooked scrambled eggs (slightly soft in the middle), berries with mint, and tiny servings of peach sorbet—one scoop for each bit of advice Clotilda had to offer.

She always had plenty of that.

"Level Four is called Survival of the Sparkliest because it's the Bests' last chance to oversee your wish-granting abilities . . . to watch you listen, plan, and use your sparkles . . . without making careless errors," she said, probably because Isabelle had already made her fair share of those. "Every single detail counts. So take my advice: If you aren't sure of something, ask. Always use formal language. When you address one of the Bests, bow your head first."

"Bow my head?" Isabelle said, nearly choking on a berry. "Even at you?"

"Especially at me." Clotilda dropped her voice to a whisper, just in case Grandmomma was snooping. "So if I were you, I wouldn't remind anyone that you waited so long to read the book. Or about the sparkles you stole and gave to Nora. Or what you did with Angelica and Fawn during the strike—if you know what I mean."

Isabelle was pretty sure "if you know what I mean" meant the orange sparkle Clotilda had given Isabelle. But maybe she meant that Isabelle shouldn't tell them about the science Clotilda had shown them. Or that she'd been to the basement to see the frogs. Or stolen a box marked DO NOT

TOUCH. Or that they'd used the sparkles they found in the box on helpless boys.

"Is Grandmomma going to join us?" Isabelle asked. (There was a lot of food.) "Or did she already leave for the center?"

A sudden burst of sparkle dust filled the air. "I'm not going to training," Grandmomma said.

Both Isabelle and Clotilda jumped. Grandmomma might be old, but she still had the ability to sneak up on her granddaughters when they were least expecting her.

"What do you mean, you're not going?" Isabelle asked.

Grandmomma put a huge stack of papers on the table. "When the terms of the negotiation were announced, a flurry of godmothers applied for retraining." She dabbed her eye. "And when I say a flurry, I mean too many to ignore for even a season."

Isabelle should have been over the moon, but she hadn't forgotten what a disaster it had been for her the last time Luciana was in charge. "You're the best teacher there is. Can't someone else help with retraining?"

Grandmomma didn't want anyone else to help. "Actually, I think this is the perfect solution. Those old godmothers can't wait to get started. And you don't need me to watch over you. Not anymore."

Clotilda gave Isabelle another extra-thick piece of French toast. But Isabelle had lost her appetite. "What makes you so sure?"

"Isabelle, you helped end the strike. You know plenty of colors. And those godmothers want me." Grand-momma's hands quivered again, probably from excitement. "You're not the only one who doesn't like waiting." Then she asked Clotilda, "Why don't you help your sister spiffy up?"

With a flick and a swoosh, magenta sparkles (for inner and outer beauty) filled the room. Isabelle began to spin, first slowly and then quickly, like a top. When the magic was finished, she was dizzy and a little bit sick to her stomach, but she looked perfect.

Now Isabelle wore a fancy new dress, slightly tight around the waist. Her hair was styled in a topknot, just like Clotilda's.

And, of course, there were new shoes. (Shoes *were* Grandmomma's favorite accessories.) In this case, her sister created brand-new green-and-yellow lace-up sneakers.

Clotilda tapped her wand to produce a full-length non-magical mirror so all three of them could marvel at her magic. "Would you look at that!" she said. "Maybe Grandmomma was right. You look cinnamon-sugar wonderful!"

Or in other words, just like Clotilda.

In the fairy godmother world, just as in the regular world, brand-new clothes can help you feel confident. Unless they're itchy. And too tight.

(Like these clothes.)

"Ow," Isabelle said. "This topknot hurts."

"It always hurts in the beginning," Clotilda said, in an annoyed tone. "Stop being a cranky pants. If it's not tight, it won't stay put. And if it doesn't stay put, you won't look official."

Isabelle wanted to look official. "But it's giving me a headache."

When Clotilda rolled her eyes, she looked exactly like Grandmomma. "I can loosen it a little, if you promise not to touch it."

Isabelle promised. But it didn't help that much. She could feel a blister forming on her big toe. Her stomach itched from the dress.

She considered asking her sister to make the sneakers a tiny bit bigger, but Clotilda was in a rush. She wouldn't want to stop to do magic. She had a meeting with the Bests.

So Isabelle tried her best to keep up and stretch out her toes at the same time. She ignored her itchy skin. She did not play with her hair.

"It's so easy for you," Isabelle told her sister. She didn't add, "And so hard for me."

Clotilda laughed. She loved flattery. "It wasn't always. But I worked hard. I didn't compare myself to everyone else. It's what I keep telling you. Learn the rules, and you will make magic."

It sounded as if it should be easy, but it wasn't. Not for Isabelle.

"Whenever I feel nervous," Clotilda continued, "I take a deep breath. I never rush. I believe in the fairy godmother mission: Happily ever after for all!" She made a heart shape with her fingers.

"And you never think of . . . her?"

Clotilda looked straight ahead. "No."

"Never?"

"What would be the point?" For a second, she looked sad, like she was taking a deep breath and waiting for the sadness to pass. "Isabelle, we can't worry about her. We can only do our jobs. Making happiness is serious business. It's a privilege and an honor and the best job in the universe. If Grandmomma thinks you were born to sparkle, you can do it." She snapped her fingers. "How could you not? You're my sister!"

"Do you mean that?"

"Absolutely," Clotilda said. Then she took off for her meeting.

Isabelle walked the rest of the way by herself. As she walked, she tried to loosen her hair. She stretched out her toes. She took out the note and reread it to make herself feel better.

But this was impossible when she could read the banners hovering above the front door to the Official Fairy Godmother Training Center.

The first message was scary: *Survival of the Sparkliest.*

Underneath that was something even worse: *May the BEST godmother win!*

Chapter Three

Catching Up with Angelica and Fawn

When Isabelle arrived at the center, Angelica and Fawn were already there.

They did not seem bothered by the banner and warnings. They didn't look nervous about training. The truth was that they looked the way they always did: studious. And responsible. And a whole lot more ready than Isabelle.

Fawn sat on the stoop by the door with her book propped open. Angelica swung from the lowest branch of the gnarly tree. They were testing one another's knowledge of blue sparkles starting with *C*, from Cambridge to Carolina, to Celeste, Cerulean, Cobalt, Columbia, and Cornflower.

There were a lot of blues.

But they didn't look frustrated. They looked as if they were having fun. As if they understood what all those shades could do. As if they were already official fairy godmothers.

When they saw Isabelle, they stopped what they were doing and the three friends embraced. "Welcome back," Isabelle said, remembering Clotilda's advice. "You both shine brightly today."

The three friends stepped back and raised their wands together, so that they pointed toward the stars. Then they admired one another's clothes and topknots. They all agreed that the hairstyle was a bit uncomfortable, but that it was worth the aggravation if it pleased Luciana.

"When I'm a Best, I will ask her to abolish dress codes," Angelica said.

"Unless I abolish them first," Fawn said.

Isabelle smiled. There was no danger of her ever becoming a Best, but for fun she said, "When I'm a Best, I'm going to bring back crowns."

In the fairy godmother world, just as in the regular one, crowns unfortunately were considered old-fashioned and totally out of style. But Isabelle didn't care. She thought they were great—loads better than topknots!

"You didn't get into trouble, did you?" Angelica asked Isabelle. "About the you-know-what." (She meant the corrupt sparkles they had used to practice their magic on boys.)

"Not *big* trouble," Isabelle said. "But I did have to apologize. More than once."

"I had to apologize five times!" Fawn said, lowering her voice. "Kaminari was sure that the sparkles belonged to your mother. And that she hid them in that box because she knew they'd lead to trouble."

Angelica agreed. "Luciana said your mother set a trap and we fell for it. She was disappointed, but couldn't totally blame us, either. So she wasn't that mad."

Even though most godmothers still believed that Mom was the worst fairy godmother ever (and capable of all kinds of shenanigans), Isabelle felt in her heart that none of them knew the whole story.

There had to be more.

"Could we make a pact not to mention my mom this level?" Isabelle asked. "Even if those sparkles did belong to her, it wasn't her fault that we used them. That's on us."

Both Fawn and Angelica looked a little bit embarrassed. It wasn't nice to speak ill of someone's mother, even if she was the worst fairy godmother in the history of all god-mothers. "Of course, you're right," Fawn said. Then she frowned. "I hope they won't use it against our overall rankings."

Angelica didn't think they would. "Luciana would have told me if she was going to dock us points." All of them knew that she was Luciana's favorite, even though Fawn (Kaminari's favorite) was ranked first.

"Did she tell you anything about that?" Isabelle asked, pointing to the banner.

Fawn laughed. "It's just a slogan," she said. "Even though, technically, we could still be sent to the Home for Normal Girls, Kaminari told me we'd have to do something even worse than . . ." She didn't finish her sentence. (Probably because she was about to say something about Mom.)

Angelica added, "Now that your grandmomma isn't going to be here, there are bound to be changes—but none that we can't handle." When Isabelle asked how she knew about Grandmomma, her friend said, "Can't you hear them?"

They stopped talking long enough for Isabelle to hear some whoops. And whistles. And funny sounds that reminded her of balloons swishing out of air. "What is that?" she asked.

"A bunch of old fairy godmothers," Fawn said. "Making mayhem."

"Mayhem?" Isabelle asked.

"Magical mayhem," Angelica whispered. "Nothing that exciting."

But Isabelle didn't believe that. "Want to go see what they're doing?"

Fawn and Angelica looked at their books. Then they shut them. Fawn said, "For all that is sparkly, let's do it!"

Isabelle took her friends by their hands, and together they ran to the other side of the center to see for themselves.

Chapter Four

Magical Mayhem

All around them—on the lawn, the steps, and even in the trees—dozens of official fairy godmothers gathered in small groups.

There were ancient godmothers doing classic old-fashioned magic, such as turning mice into horses.

There were somewhat-old fairy godmothers making accessories such as magic roses and slippers and sewing materials.

And there were others of all ages hanging around a large makeshift tent next to a heavily stocked frog pond. A few godmothers catapulted sparkles into the sky for absolutely no reason at all.

Tossing sparkles into the sky was dangerous and wasteful. Even Isabelle knew that.

Minerva, Irene, and MaryEllen must have known that, too, because they were running as fast as they could, distracting the old godmothers with large trays of food from every corner of the regular world: There were empanadas filled with meat, grilled fish with Japanese pickles on the side, and a big bowl of shakshuka, which was a dish made with tomatoes, eggs, onions, and melted feta cheese.

Angelica rubbed her tummy. "Let's get something to eat."

But the second the old godmothers spotted the three trainees, they stopped what they were doing and swarmed Isabelle.

They kissed her hands and the hem of her dress. They bowed their heads to her—as if she were a Best.

It was very embarrassing.

"Please stop," Isabelle said. "I'm not a Best. I don't deserve this."

But they thought she was just being humble. "Last night," an old fairy godmother said, "Minerva told us all about you, and how you ended the strike all by yourself. She told us you are going to go down in history as one of the best fairy godmothers ever."

"She did?" Angelica and Fawn asked. They looked mildly peeved. At Isabelle.

And to make it even worse, the godmothers gave her presents.

The first gift came from the shortest, most ancient and wrinkly godmother Isabelle had ever seen—even more ancient and wrinkly and stooped than Minerva and Zahara combined.

"Isabelle, I made Jacques for you," she said, pointing to a beautiful brown-and-black horse (that obviously used to be a mouse). "His great-great-great-great-great-great-great- (plus a few more greats) grandmother was one of the originals."

Isabelle didn't need to ask whom she was referring to. "Thank you very much."

The godmother handed Isabelle the reins. "It's been a long time since I felt brave enough to ask for a modern princess. But now that I can go back to training, I'm ready to wave my wand and share the sparkle!" She asked the horse to take a knee so Isabelle could scratch his head, but when she did, the horse disappeared into a cloud of sparkles. Now at her feet, Isabelle stared at Jacques—the mouse.

Fawn screamed. (She was afraid of mice.)

Isabelle knelt down and told the mouse to go to the castle basement. When she stood up, another very old godmother (but not quite as old as the last one) stepped forward with a small wrapped box, which unfortunately turned out to be a rule book.

Isabelle said, "Thank you, but I have one of these."

The godmother thrust it into her hands. "Not like this, you don't."

It was an original rule book, first edition. This *was* a treasure!

The book was brittle and it smelled a bit moldy—it had probably been sitting in the godmother's basement for a long time—so Isabelle turned the pages very slowly and carefully. Most of the rules were written with beautiful swirling letters.

Rules like:

Gold can make a princess stubborn.

Don't forget to write down all your ratios.

Avoid using black and red together unless three godmothers have approved your proportions.

In the margin, there were more notes, all written by hand and decorated with swirlies and hearts and squares. One in particular caught her eye:

If red offers power and black offers knowledge, why won't they let us combine them? This seems to be an obvious way to get to happily ever after. Must do more research! If I do this, I could be #1!

Isabelle closed the book and tucked it under her arm. Remember: Fairy godmothers didn't believe in coincidences. In other words, this advice was meant for her.

Her friends, however, were extremely curious and persistent. "Give it here," Angelica said. "I've never seen an original."

Fawn thought Isabelle should hand it over to the Bests. "These rules might be outdated."

For a second, Isabelle wondered whether this book had been Mom's—but then she remembered that the rule book was written because of Mom, after she'd been banished. Even so, there was no way Isabelle was going to hand it in. It was a great gift—one that might help her survive training!

She turned to thank the godmother who gave it to her, but the old wand-waver was gone. In her place was a younger fairy godmother with a less controversial gift. It was a pair of monogrammed goggles, just like the kind Fawn and Angelica owned.

When Isabelle put them on, her glasses fogged up, but only for a few seconds. "How did you know I wanted these?" Isabelle asked.

The fairy godmother smiled. She pointed to a crowd of godmothers moving slowly toward them. "From Zahara."

Grandmomma's ex–best friend was still very popular, especially after standing up to the Bests in the strike.

Zahara handed Isabelle a small wrapped box. "A few of us polished this up last night. Everyone thought you deserved it." She added, "It was mine once."

Isabelle opened the box as quickly as she could. Inside was a famous piece of jewelry passed down from the very first godmothers. It was a badge the size of the star on her wand. It was shaped like an apple and decorated with many jewels, including a big silver *#1* smack in the middle.

Now Angelica and Fawn looked more than peeved. They looked downright insulted.

It was a bit awkward.

Actually more than a bit.

But Zahara didn't care. "Put it on," she said. "It will look perfect on your collar." As Isabelle did what she was told (it wasn't wise to ignore the wishes of ancient godmothers), Zahara whispered, "If you twist the stem three times to the right, you'll find a little compartment holding a couple of sparkles. For a rainy day!"

Secret sparkles were nice, but this honor was very embarrassing, since Isabelle ranked no better than the third-best trainee. But if she put it in her pocket or gave it to Fawn, that would be rude.

Fairy godmothers could be a lot of things—powerful, ambitious, mushy—but when it came to accepting presents, they tried never to be ungracious.

So Isabelle thanked Zahara, while at the same time hoping that Luciana wouldn't notice it on her collar. She also hoped that the pin was the last of the gifts.

Also, she wanted one more second to look at that old book. She couldn't stop thinking about all the good things red and black sparkles could do. She also couldn't stop thinking that using them would show Luciana, Raine, and

Kaminari that she was the boldest and sparkliest of all the trainees—which seemed to be the point of this level.

But then Grandmomma arrived in a dark purple all-terrain vehicle that had definitely once been an eggplant. When she stepped out, she embraced Zahara. Then she asked the group of old godmothers, "Are you ready to go back to school?"

When they cheered, giant pale-green snowflakes fell from the sky.

Godmothers old and young stuck out their tongues. "Isn't this wonderful?" Fawn cried. Isabelle and Angelica had to agree. The snowflakes tasted like peppermint!

Magic was literally in the air.

That meant it was time to return to the Official Fairy Godmother Training Center!

Angelica and Fawn started to run—they hated to be late—but then they stopped, because Isabelle didn't want to leave the Grands behind.

She told them all to link arms the way Nora and her friends Samantha, Janet, and Mason did when they were extra happy. She said, "Let's walk together! This *is* the last time!"

Since she was right (for once), they did it. They walked in sync, smiling all the way to the "ready" door.

Irene invited everyone to huddle together. "This is it, ladies!"

MaryEllen smiled. "The moment has arrived."

Minerva whispered to Isabelle, "Were you surprised?"

Isabelle thanked her, even though she still thought the presents were unnecessary.

Minerva disagreed. "Keep listening to your heart, Isabelle. No matter how many tricks we learn, that's the fastest way to make happily ever after."

Isabelle held the old rule book tightly. So far, she felt great. Everything was going really well.

There was only one thing missing.

Minerva knew Isabelle too well. She whispered, "Wherever she is, your mom is proud of you."

Chapter Five

There's Always a *But*

When Isabelle stepped over the threshold into the training center, she was expecting to see the usual setup of desks and chairs, a few slogans and pictures, and Grandmomma's desk.

But today, everything was different.

The desks and chairs they had sat in were gone. Most of the slogans were gone. Now there were tables displaying equipment for scientifically combining sparkles. A giant spectrum of sparkles beamed across the back wall. All the trainees (and especially the Grands) shielded their eyes from the brightness.

Once their eyes adjusted, they could see that a few things had been left alone. Isabelle's favorite sign, HAPPILY EVER AFTER: THE LAST LINE OF EVERY GREAT STORY, still hung on the front wall, but now it hung under a brand-new plaque, KEEP CALM AND SPARKLE ON. There were a few pictures from last night's Extravaganza, and the Bests had even made a small tribute to the strike—two framed signs, FIGHT LIKE A GODMOTHER and RESPECT THE POWER OF THE SPARKLE—and a framed picture of Isabelle, Minerva, and Grandmomma. Isabelle burst into giggles (and relief) when she found the class picture on the center of the wall. In the photo, Fawn held bunny ears behind her head.

"Angelica dared me," she told Isabelle. She looked a bit embarrassed. "Sorry."

"It's okay." That was the kind of dare that didn't bother Isabelle. It was a joke between friends.

But the rest of the room was no joke. Every other free space was covered with warnings like:

Don't touch without permission.
Wear protective gear at all times.
Work alone! You are not here to make friends.

While Isabelle tried to imagine what size protective gear they'd need to fit over their puffy dresses, Angelica pointed to the sand-colored "emergency wands" in every corner of the room. "Luciana told me that they're filled with powerful sparkles that neutralize—in other words, undo—magical disasters. If we hear an alarm, we must break the seal, pull the safety pin, and aim."

Isabelle was about to ask how they were supposed to break a magic seal in the middle of an emergency (even though she was 99.9 percent sure it was in the book), when the door swung open to a loud chorus of trumpets.

Isabelle rubbed her stomach, even though she was still full and her dress was too tight. She couldn't help it. The Bests didn't just arrive with great fanfare. They always brought food.

But not this time.

Today, the Bests wore jackets and slacks and starched white shirts, each representing a different part of the regular world.

Luciana's suit was the same blue as the flag of Argentina, the home of her first princess. Raine's was red, yellow, and green, like the flag of Ethiopia—and her shoes were encrusted with jewels of the same colors. Kaminari wore a crimson-red suit that matched the flag of Japan. Clotilda had changed out of her dress and into a blue pantsuit with a red-and-white blouse, in honor of her first princess, Melody, from America.

Isabelle tugged at the pin in her hair. The Bests looked modern and comfortable—so much better than the fussy dress Clotilda had given her.

Luciana winked, as though she could tell what Isabelle was thinking. "It's so nice to see all of you here today. First and foremost, I want to congratulate you for making it this far—and maybe more important, for showing us your gusto during the strike. You have all come a long way, and we are very excited to see the fine work you will surely do in the future."

She walked around the room so that each trainee could bow her head in her direction.

"During Level One, we watched you learn to think on your feet and develop your signature styles. In Level Two, we tested your strength and dexterity, and you persevered through unusual circumstances . . . with less than optimal materials." Then she stopped walking and pointed her wand at the Grands. "And you taught us a lot, too, ladies. About fairness. And experience. And how some habits and rules that worked for a while can get very stale if they are not revisited."

"So, with that in mind," Raine said, "we are delighted to

tell you that during this level, there will be no tricks or advantages."

Kaminari added, "All of you will be given the most optimal situations and complete access to maximum sparkles."

This was exactly what the trainees had been wishing for!

But then it came.

The *but*.

Of course, from none other than Clotilda. "But that doesn't mean Level Four is going to be a cakewalk." She cleared her throat. "With maximum sparkle power comes maximum sparkle responsibility. You have to stay on your toes. You have to correct your mistakes. You have to speak up if you are confused."

As Clotilda continued to ruin the mood, Isabelle doodled an unflattering picture of her sister in her notebook. She didn't like when the Bests talked about mistakes, because it meant that everyone was thinking about Mom.

Thinking about Mom made her collar itch more than ever. Her feet felt hot. She tried to loosen her hair, but

Clotilda's magic was impossible to overcome. Every time she tugged on a pin, it tightened even more.

"Isabelle?" Luciana prompted. Her eyes looked like fire. "Are you with us?"

Obviously, she wasn't.

Luciana looked peeved. "Your sister just asked how you would approach your first princess today." Before Isabelle could slump lower into her seat, Luciana asked, "Since you are wearing a Number One jewel, you can go first. Tell us, if you could do it all over again, what would you do differently?"

Isabelle scratched her neck. "Well, since Nora became my princess before she had ever made a wish or even realized that fairy godmothers were real, I would definitely wait and listen longer before going to meet her." She sighed, because she hated waiting—since you never knew how long it would last. She also hated Rule Three C (as well as all the fine print) and was about to ask why they insisted on keeping this rule, but then she didn't—they were never going to change it. So she made another suggestion. "Can we change out of these dresses? I'd really like to wear clothes like yours." She tried not to look at Clotilda (who was probably furious). "This topknot is unbearable!"

Luciana shrugged. "That's not a terrible idea." She flicked her wand and changed their dresses into comfortable clothes.

Isabelle couldn't help herself. She jumped up and shouted, "Thank you, Luciana! You're the best!" Then she gave the Number One fairy godmother a kiss on each cheek.

For the record, in the fairy godmother world, jumping up and kissing the cheeks of the Number One fairy godmother was pretty much unacceptable—even more so than daydreaming in class. Everyone started snickering.

Raine tapped her wand until order had been restored. "Waiting for your princess to make a great wish is particularly important because today, more than ever before, princesses have power. They have influence. They hold important jobs. Most of all, they care deeply about causes that require great thought."

"You mean I was right?" Isabelle said. She started to twirl—and maybe give Luciana another unnecessary kiss on the check—but then she stopped. She sat back down.

Angelica gave her two thumbs up. Then she raised her hand. "You know what they say: Sparkly things come to those who wait."

As the rest of the godmothers pondered the joys of listening and patience, Isabelle drew a big swirl in her notebook. Listening and waiting. Waiting and listening. No matter how much sparkle they promised, they always said the same thing.

Fawn jumped in next. "It's also our job to use this time to look ahead, to think about everything that might happen once a princess's wish comes true. We must listen to what our princesses want and also listen to the world, so we can see what they need to make the world a better place."

Isabelle popped to attention. "Making the world a better place was what Nora wanted, too."

She might have said more about Nora but then Minerva stood up. The last time she did this, a strike started, so this time, everyone immediately gave her the floor. "Patience is also an essential element of trust—the foundation of the relationship between godmother and princess." She looked to Irene, who added, "Just like our time together helps all of us trust each other, our time with our princesses assures them that they can trust us."

"So when things get tough," MaryEllen said, "they do not lose all hope."

Luciana clapped her hands. "As one of my favorite princesses once told me: 'If you don't study the mistakes of the past, you are doomed to repeat them.'"

That sounded scary. (It was supposed to.)

Clotilda said, with a smile on her face, "So let's get started. Today we are going to give you one of the most difficult wishes in fairy godmother history. And we want to see how you would grant it."

In other words, testing was about to begin.

Chapter Six

May the Best Godmother Win!

When everyone was dressed in head-to-toe protective gear, gold papers just like the one Grandmomma gave Isabelle appeared in front of each trainee.

Luciana said, "What you have in front of you is the beginning of the story of a very famous princess. I will add that this wish could have gone terribly wrong, but thanks to the kindness, determination, and gusto of her fairy godmother, this princess became happily ever after."

That was exciting.

It meant this princess was definitely in the book.

Raine said, "Today, we would like each of you to come up with a plan of action for granting this historic wish." Kaminari pointed around the room to their books as well as a wall of classic and modern accessories and the science station, where they could find the spectrum of sparkles in vacuum-sealed containers.

Clotilda looked straight at Isabelle. "Before you begin, do you have any questions?"

Isabelle had a gazillion questions. Like how long they had to complete the task, and whether it mattered who finished first. (She was thinking about the *Survival of the Sparkliest* banner.) She also wanted to know if there was anything they couldn't do besides use orange sparkles. And if they messed up, how many times could they start over? But when neither the Grands nor Angelica nor Fawn raised their hands, she didn't raise hers either.

Clotilda smiled. "Okay, then. Let's begin. May the best godmother win!"

Isabelle turned the page over. She was happy to see that there was no fine print and that the story was short.

Once upon a time, there was a king, a queen, and a princess named ■■■■ *[Name Redacted]. Even though she was the smartest and most admired princess in all the lands, she was most unhappy. Also, she had magical powers of her own.*

Isabelle took her time. She wrote down:

Only child.
Very smart.
Lots of responsibility.
Magical princess. Must have lived a long time ago.

Then she kept reading.

The king and queen gave her everything she asked for, from ponies to long vacations, to books and snacks and festivals in her name. But she remained miserable. They were convinced she was unhappy because she was lonely. Unfortunately, every time they introduced her to anyone, she turned the

poor prince or princess into a frog or a lizard or other
random amphibian.

When word got out about the amphibians and reptiles, no
one wanted to go near the castle. No one wanted to speak to the
princess. As time passed, no one would even work at the castle.
The grounds were ignored. Ivy covered the castle. No one
would go in or out.

The entire world was afraid of the princess.

So her mother, now very old and all out of answers, called
the fairy godmother.

Maybe the story was too short.

Isabelle thought it over. It seemed obvious that the princess wanted to rule the world more than she wanted friends—that power (and power alone) would make her happily ever after.

In other words, the old book was spot on. Black and red sparkles would definitely do the trick!

But that seemed awfully easy.

Like trick-question easy.

So Isabelle thought about it some more and then even longer, until the words looked blurry and her legs felt stiff and she couldn't sit another second. Maybe this wasn't a trick. Maybe the king and queen were wrong about their daughter.

Who were they to judge?

She was just about to stand up and gather some sparkles when she heard someone whisper her name. But she must have been mistaken, because when she looked around, everyone was busy reading or taking notes or gathering sparkles. No one was even looking at her.

Maybe she was just nervous. Imagining things.

But no. When she stood up, there it was again. This time louder.

"Isabelle! Stop!"

This was very unnerving. And confusing, too. Isabelle wondered if the other trainees were hearing things, too. If so, this could be part of the test. The voice—whoever it was—could be misleading her or helping her. She didn't know what she should do.

The voice sounded desperate. "Before you settle on sparkles, look in your Wish List."

This was an undeniably good idea, so Isabelle went back to her seat and opened the book. She found the section on princesses who wished for power. But to her dismay, the section was long. Not only that, but there was a great deal of fine print and more than two hundred footnotes.

In other words, a lot of princesses wanted power.

Some princesses wanted power and love. Some wanted power and friendship. One princess needed a fuzzy pet to make her happily ever after; power wasn't really all that important at all.

But that was just the beginning.

Princesses wanted knowledge and power for tons of reasons. In the old days, there was a lot of discovering new lands or leading revolutions. Some princesses wanted to make laws more fair. Helping others was a big motivation. So was scientific discovery. Others wanted to make beautiful art.

Isabelle felt lost. She didn't know what to do.

So she did what she always did, but shouldn't. She looked around the room to see what the other trainees were doing. (She was sure they'd all been given the same problem princess.)

Angelica was using her wand to combine her sparkles in a tall drinking glass.

Fawn had turned her wand into a giant needle and was sewing her sparkles into a beautiful gown. (That was so creative.) Isabelle could see that she'd taken a whole bunch of vacuum-sealed containers, including some darker colors and pink. From where she sat, it looked as though Minerva was baking.

Isabelle couldn't stop thinking about the old rule book. (Remember: Fairy godmothers did not believe in coincidences. Also: Remembering one line was a lot easier than reading any more fine print.)

With as much confidence as possible, Isabelle headed to the table filled with sparkles and took two huge packages of red and black.

Then, because her friends had taken other colors, she grabbed some extra orange and a handful of pink for humor, and a tiny bit of gold for determination—but only a tiny bit, because a girl who would turn potential friends into amphibians and reptiles was probably stubborn enough. She also got some light blue and some chartreuse, even though she still didn't know how to pronounce it.

She was just about to start mixing when the whisper told her, "Not so much red. Put the black sparkles down."

Isabelle wished the whisper would go away. She figured it had to be a trick. She remembered the warning: She wasn't here to make friends.

When Luciana told them, "Ten more minutes," Isabelle finalized her plan: She was going to infuse the sparkle power into the tiara and give it (hypothetically) to the princess.

As Clotilda would say, easy peasy lemon squeezy!

Or as the voice said, "No, Isabelle! The old book is wrong! Don't!"

But Isabelle wasn't listening anymore.

As quickly as she could, Isabelle added the sparkles to her colorimeter and stirred the combination together.

It made a sizzle sound. And a pop.

Isabelle loved it! Her sparkles felt alive!

Next, she packed as many of those sparkles as she could into her wand. When her wand was sealed and ready to go, she pointed it straight at the tiara for maximum sparkle power. And then she thought very deeply about happiness. And power. And of course, strength, knowledge, and friendship. And then she thought about how great it would be to be the best godmother in the class, and how she couldn't wait to see Nora. And right away, the tiara glowed and shined and began to spin in the air.

Isabelle felt a bit smug.

But Fawn looked scared. "Isabelle! Your tiara! What did you do?"

Angelica stepped out of the way. "That doesn't look safe!"

At first, Isabelle was sure that Fawn and Angelica were jealous, but then the tiara wouldn't stop spinning. Instead of slowing down, it began to swell and steam as if the sparkles were hot and wanted to escape.

Isabelle grabbed some potholders and tossed the tiara into a safety cabinet. She slammed the cabinet door shut. She hoped that after a few moments, the magic would settle down and that no one else would notice.

But just in case it didn't, she motioned to her sister. "Clotilda, I think I stuffed my wand with too many sparkles!"

It was too late! Before Clotilda could grab one of those sand-colored wands from a corner of the room (or even before she could say, "For all that is sparkly"), the cabinet doors burst open! The tiara soared into the center of the room and spit sparkles into every corner. Alarms blared. The tiara looked like fire. The room began to fill with sparkle dust!

Kaminari shouted, "Duck for cover!"

Luciana shouted, "Run for your lives!"

In record time, the trainees and Grands ran toward the gnarly tree so they could wait for the magic to simmer down. The Bests stood like guards with their wands pointed at every window and door. They looked as though they were using every muscle in their bodies. Their wands shot protective sparkles at the building.

Fawn covered her eyes.

Angelica glared at Isabelle.

The Grands said, "This does not look good."

Giant puffs of pink, red, and orange streamed out the windows. Streaks of sparkles bounced from one wall to another. The whole building shuddered and quaked and hissed with sparkle overload as if it had been hit by a gigantic sparkly rainbow.

This wasn't any sparkle mess. This was a sparkle disaster.

Even worse, it was all Isabelle's fault.

Chapter Seven

The Worst Sparkle Disaster Ever!

The Bests wanted to know everything. Every move. Every decision. Every detail. This was standard procedure after a sparkle disaster.

They asked Isabelle:

"What sparkles did you use?"

"How many did you take?"

"How quickly did you combine them?"

Isabelle told them *almost* everything. "Because the princess wanted to be left alone, I made a combination of mostly red and black sparkles, but I also used a tiny bit of pink and yellow and blue." Then she thought about it. "And some gold. And the neat yellow-green one."

"You mean chartreuse?"

Isabelle nodded. "Yes, chartreuse." (Now she knew how to pronounce it: "shar-*truce*.")

Clotilda couldn't stand still. "And nothing else? Are you sure about that, Isabelle?"

Isabelle nodded again. "No. Nothing else." She added, "Mostly, I used red and black."

When the Bests heard "mostly red and black," they looked at each other with very grim expressions. They shook their heads in dismay. "How much red? How much black?"

Isabelle wished she could be exact, but she hadn't exactly measured. She said, "Can there be too much knowledge and power?" When they frowned, she said, "There wasn't much to go on."

Clotilda threw up her hands in utter despair. "Isabelle! What were you thinking? Did you even look in your books?" Then she said the worst possible thing: "You did what Mom would have done."

Luciana, Raine, and Kaminari agreed. "That's exactly what she would have done."

"Why is that so bad?" Isabelle begged her sister to explain. "In the old book, it recommended that combination."

Luciana looked as red as the reddest sparkle. "In what old book?"

Isabelle took the book out from under her protective gear. "It was a gift. For ending the strike." But when she turned to the page with the handwritten notes, everything looked different. Now she read:

WARNING!
Extremely Important Notes on Using High Quantities of Dangerous Sparkles, especially Black and Red at the Exact Same Time Without Measuring.

Clotilda walked away.

"Isabelle," Fawn said. "I don't know what to say." She tried to peek into the window, but there was too much dust for anyone to see anything.

"She's even worse than her mother," Angelica muttered.

Isabelle couldn't take her eyes off the book. "But this isn't what it said," she told them. "I think someone's played a trick on me." But her friends didn't seem to be listening.

Luciana handed Isabelle a broom and a dustpan and some brand-new protective gear, including special gloves and a mask to cover her nose and mouth so she wouldn't breathe in any sparkle fumes. She told everyone else to go home.

Once they were gone, she pointed to the "not ready" door. "Isabelle, go inside and clean up this mess."

When Isabelle entered the center, she wanted to cry. (But she didn't. She was determined to hold it in.) Every surface, from the floor to every table, chair, and display, wasn't just covered with red, yellow, blue, and every other color of sparkle soot imaginable. It was *buried* in every color of sparkle soot imaginable.

Beakers lay smashed on the floor.

The walls were streaked with dust.

All of the signs and slogans and photos from the last Extravaganza had fallen to the floor.

Worst of all, her favorite sign, HAPPILY EVER AFTER: THE LAST LINE OF EVERY GREAT STORY, was ruined, splintered right down the center.

Luciana picked up the pieces of the sign and tossed them into the trash. She looked more like an evil stepmother than a godmother in charge of training.

"Are you sure we can't use magic to clean up this mess?" Isabelle asked.

Unfortunately, Luciana was not a fairy godmother who ever used sparkles when slow, hard, painful work could get the job done. "No. You have wasted enough sparkles for one day. You need to clean this up the old-fashioned way."

So Isabelle picked up the broom and started sweeping. And sweeping. And sweeping. And it wasn't easy.

When she pressed hard on the broom, the soot streaked. It got stuck in every crack. When she used a lighter touch, sparkles swirled into the air like a cloud. And when she pressed somewhere in the middle, not much happened at all.

It was really discouraging.

But since there was no point in complaining, she did the best she could.

She swept up as much as possible into a dustpan, then she started again, and another time after that. When she got down to a thin layer of streaky, colorful soot, she used a wet mop, and when she got tired of that, she wiped off all the surfaces and counters with a sponge.

As she worked, she thought of all the famous princesses who had also been cleaner-uppers. She couldn't understand what the appeal was. All this work didn't make her want to sing. Or dream. Or make a wish other than to be done and go to bed. If a bluebird wanted to rest on her shoulder, she would not have been amused.

When she was finally done—when the center was as clean as it had been before class began, and her arms were sore and her hands ached—she called to Luciana, Raine, and Kaminari to come inspect.

They all wore white gloves.

None of them were pleased.

Isabelle bowed her head. "I have learned my lesson." When they didn't move, she added, "Next time, I will read the entire document before I start my magic. I will not be distracted by any old books or notes or anything else that doesn't make sense. Next time, I promise I will make you proud."

Every time she said "Next time," Luciana flinched. Raine shook her head. Kaminari muttered, "For all that is sparkly," but didn't finish her sentence.

"This isn't working for us," Luciana said. "Even though we wanted to believe that you could become an official fairy godmother, it is now clear that we were right all along. We can't trust you, not with a wand. Not with a princess. And definitely not with sparkles." She paused so it could all sink in. "Isabelle, we are sorry to say we have to say good-bye and good luck. Be assured we did the best we could."

"What are you saying?" Isabelle said.

Luciana held out her hand for Isabelle's wand. And then she ripped the Number One pin (with the secret sparkles) from Zahara off Isabelle's collar and put it in her pocket. "Isabelle, using red and black together is not a forgivable offense. Therefore, we must officially pronounce that you have flunked out of the Official Fairy Godmother Training Center. We hope you find a better purpose at the Fairy Godmother Home for Normal Girls. Pack up your books and go."

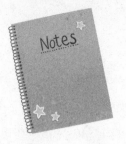

Chapter Eight

Back to the Basement

Isabelle walked out the door and down the path to Grandmomma's castle.

She was, understandably, not in a rush.

There would be no easy way to tell Grandmomma she was going to the Fairy Godmother Home for Normal Girls. It was where, if Isabelle were being honest, she'd always believed she would end up. It was where trainees who didn't concentrate or read the fine print or follow the rules belonged.

She walked down the path as if this were her last time. She noticed the flowers and the birds and all the small, cute animals that lived in the fairy godmother world. She noticed how beautiful the front of the castle looked. And as she walked through the foyer, up the stairs, and down the hall to Grandmomma's office, she noticed, maybe for the first time, how many beautiful paintings hung on the walls. Last but not least, she admired the doorknocker, a lion with its mouth wide open. Today, it didn't look angry. Instead, it looked as sad as she felt.

Before she could knock, Grandmomma said, "Come in."

Isabelle opened the door.

Clotilda and Grandmomma were standing behind Grandmomma's desk with their hands on their hips. They were clearly waiting for her.

"Did you tell Grandmomma what happened?" Isabelle asked.

Her sister's cheeks were almost the same color as the tiara right before it exploded. "Do you realize how embarrassing this is? For me? And Grandmomma? For the entire fairy godmother world that trusted you with this opportunity and didn't once complain that you had already messed up a whole bunch of times?"

Isabelle wished she could simply pack her bags and go. "You don't have to say it. I'm as bad as Mom. Maybe even worse."

When no one disagreed, she noticed something else. The office looked different. At first she wondered whether Grandmomma had magically made it bigger. But then she noticed the dark shadows on the floor.

The magic mirror was gone. So was the spinning wheel. And so was the spyglass.

"Did I get you in trouble, too?" Isabelle asked. Grandmomma loved her spyglass. Her mirror and spinning wheel were important fairy godmother antiques.

This day was getting even worse than worst!

Before either sister could say anything, Grandmomma asked Clotilda to leave. "Isabelle and I have a lot to discuss. I hope you understand."

Clotilda glared at Isabelle on her way out the door. "Of

course, I understand." She didn't have to add: She was the good sister.

Grandmomma stood still until it was clear that Clotilda was not listening from the other side of the wall. Then she gestured for Isabelle to come closer.

"I promise I'm not going to scold you." She dropped her voice to a whisper. "If you do what I say, everything is going to be fine."

Isabelle knew that *fine* was another word for "not great." Or "fairly awful." But since it also meant not totally disastrous, she took a deep breath and sat down.

"Did they take your things because of me?" Isabelle asked.

"They did not," Grandmomma said.

"Do I need to pack for the Home right now?"

Grandmomma looked at her sternly. "No, you do not. Unless that's where you want to go."

"What do you mean, 'unless'?" Isabelle asked.

Grandmomma warned Isabelle that what she was about to say could never be repeated, even to Clotilda. And that if anyone—especially Clotilda—found out, she would know that it was Isabelle who spilled the beans, and she would regret it.

"Do we understand each other?"

Isabelle, of course, said, "I understand." This was Grandmomma—with the emphasis on *grand*. (Also, she was really scared.)

"Then let's go to the basement. There is something important I need to show you."

Getting to the basement was always a little bit of a production, but it took even longer because Grandmomma moved slowly. She dressed slowly. She walked down the spiral stairs slowly.

But, slowly but surely, they got there.

"What do you have to show me? What did you do with your stuff? What do you mean, I don't have to go to the Home?" Honestly, there was nothing worse than waiting!

Grandmomma tapped her wand on the wall. Right away, her desk appeared. So did the rickety chair for Isabelle.

"How much do you know?" Isabelle asked.

"Everything," Grandmomma said. And she didn't raise her wand.

Isabelle tried to relax. "So you know about the voice I heard? Does that mean it was you?"

Grandmomma shook her head. "No it wasn't." Then she sat forward in her chair. "Let's talk about that voice. Did she sound nice? Young? Funny? Sad?"

Isabelle thought about that. "Actually, the voice seemed gentle. And smart. And sweet. But not as sweet as Clotilda."

"So then why didn't you listen?"

Isabelle sighed. "I thought it was a trick—that the voice was trying to fool me. I was so sure it was part of the test. That the old rule book had all the right answers."

Apparently, Grandmomma had heard enough, because she told Isabelle to stand. Then she said the one thing Isabelle was not expecting to hear.

"That book belonged to me."

"You?" Isabelle said. "Are you saying you sabotaged my sparkle? That you wanted me to fail?"

Grandmomma looked very offended. "I would never sabotage a sparkle. But I did give you that book with the bad advice. And I will also admit that I wanted to see what would happen if you found yourself in trouble." Grandmomma rolled her eyes. "But it's not my fault you fell for it."

"But why would you do that?" Isabelle asked. "Did you really not want me to be a fairy godmother?"

In the dim basement light, Grandmomma looked more exhausted than grand. "I did it because I wanted to see whether your mother would attempt to come back to help you. I wanted proof that she was watching you and that if you got in trouble, she would save you. But judging by what you're telling me, she can't do it. Maybe she's grown too weak. Or maybe she doesn't have enough sparkle left herself."

Isabelle couldn't believe it. "That was my mom?"

Grandmomma nodded. "That was her. Smartest godmother I ever raised."

Isabelle felt slightly dizzy. All this time, her mother had been watching and trying to help her. It wasn't just her imagination. "But I thought Mom couldn't come back—that you took all her sparkles."

Grandmomma looked very serious. "Technically, we did, but it isn't that hard to steal sparkles—if you really want them."

Isabelle had to admit that stealing sparkles *was* pretty easy. She also remembered when Grandmomma left training during Level Two. "You were looking for her then?"

Grandmomma nodded. "Isabelle, I don't know what you've heard, but fairy godmothers are never vengeful or spiteful or mean." She opened her Wish List and paged through the book. "I'm sorry I had to disrupt your training, but I had to try."

Isabelle totally understood. "So now that your plan didn't work, can you tell Luciana? So I can go back to training?"

Grandmomma shook her head. "No. I'm sorry. I can't do that."

"Why not?" Isabelle asked.

"Because you have a more important job to do. Now that you are out of the system, we can work together—in secret. We can find your mom and bring her home. We can end the unhappy princess's story the way it should have ended— with a real happily ever after."

This sounded spectacular! But also difficult.

"How are we going to do that?" Isabelle asked.

Grandmomma pointed her wand at one of the large boxes in the corner. Immediately, the top opened up and a small box marked with a *V* emerged and sailed across the room onto her desk. "Open it. This is all we have to go on."

Inside were three bags of unsealed sparkles and a photograph.

The first bag contained the brightest sparkles Isabelle had ever seen—so bright she needed sunglasses to examine them! They looked like sunlight and moonlight and every star in the sky. An entire prism of color all contained in one sparkle.

"Wow."

Grandmomma agreed they were amazing to look at, but after all this time, useless. (So she shouldn't bother pocketing them.) "Starlike sparkles make very strong magic because they encompass the entire spectrum of light. When you use sparkles with this much power, there is no turning back."

"What do you mean?" Isabelle asked.

"These sparkles create a bond that can never be broken."

Now Isabelle felt a bit let down. "A bond that couldn't be broken" didn't sound so bad! But it must have been, because Grandmomma pounded her fist on the table. She told Isabelle to take this seriously. She added, "When you use sparkles this strong, there is no turning back."

Grandmomma showed her the second packet. This one held old aquamarine sparkles, also out of date.

Isabelle peeked in her book. "Those sparkles are for healing."

Grandmomma nodded. "They work especially well on a broken heart."

The third held a few remnants of black and red.

"Can you guess why your mother might have had these?" Grandmomma asked.

"I bet she wanted to override Rule Three C."

"That's what I thought at first," Grandmomma said. "Hypothetically, knowledge and power could do it. But she didn't combine knowledge and power and healing for that. She did it for selfish reasons." Grandmomma paused. "For herself."

"What do you mean, for herself?" Isabelle asked.

"Your mother might have been powerful and talented, but she was also proud. She refused to let anyone else even try to help her make that princess happily ever after. When it was clear that she had failed, she used those sparkles to hide the princess away so none of us could hear her. Or find her. Or help her. So that the princess couldn't find happiness from anyone but your mother."

Isabelle needed a moment to let it all sink in. "You can do that? With those sparkles?" Even she had to admit that seemed very selfish.

Grandmomma sulked. "As I said, she was a very powerful godmother. If she would have asked for some help, she could have made many princesses happy."

Isabelle picked up the photograph. "So this is her?" she asked. "The princess?"

The young woman in the picture didn't look like the princesses from the Wish List. First of all, she wasn't wearing a crown. Her clothes were plain. She looked as if she were trying not to look sad, but couldn't completely hide it. Although Isabelle was sure she'd never seen her face before, she thought the woman looked weirdly familiar, but she couldn't say why.

Grandmomma shook her head. "I don't know who that is. I don't know if the picture means anything! All I know: It belonged to your mother. When we banished her, we found it with her sparkles."

Now Isabelle was annoyed. And confused. And curious. And excited.

She was annoyed and confused because, obviously, this wasn't going to be easy. The sparkles made sense, but the picture did not. She was also curious about Mom and how things had gotten this bad. And, of course, excited because for the first time ever, Grandmomma needed her. She trusted her to help find Mom.

But there was one thing she needed to know. "Can you tell me the real story of the unhappy princess?" She added, "The whole story. And whatever you do, don't leave anything out."

Chapter Nine

The Official Story of the Unhappy
Princess, According to Grandmomma.
Plus, Something Even Sadder
(If You Can Believe That).

Grandmomma looked as if she didn't want to tell this story. But she knew that Isabelle couldn't help her unless she heard the whole truth and nothing but the truth.

Grandmomma reminded her, "Everything else you learned from earlier books was wrong. Or tainted by gossip."

Just in case you don't remember:

Clotilda's version blamed the princess in *The Wish List #1: The Worst Fairy Godmother Ever!*

In *The Wish List #2: Keep Calm and Sparkle On!*, Angelica put all the blame on Mom.

And in *The Wish List #3: Halfway to Happily Ever After*, Minerva skewered the system.

Now it was time for the truth.

Once upon a time, your mother became a brand-new fairy godmother. She displayed excellent skills with her wand. She was everything that a great fairy godmother should be. Kind. Determined. And overflowing with gusto. We had great expectations for her. We were sure she would soon be a Best.

At the same time, a lovely princess came of age. Not only

was she royal, but she was also a good person, the most beloved princess in all the land.

Even better, this princess had fallen in love. And made a wish.

Easy peasy, or so it seemed.

Right after your mom introduced herself, the princess changed her mind about what she wanted to wish for. And then she changed her mind again. And again! She wouldn't settle on a single wish! But your mother was wise and powerful, and like all great fairy godmothers, she did not fret. While the princess tried to figure out what she wanted, your mother waited. She listened. When we asked what was going on, your mother defended the princess. She told us that the princess was only unhappy because she didn't want to be pushed into making a decision.

For a while, the Bests let them be. But eventually it was clear that the princess wasn't just indecisive. She was unhappy. The regular world could see it, too. So we decided to replace your mother with a fairy godmother with more experience. We didn't think it was that big a deal. Fairy godmothers helped each other all the time. In this case, we assured your mother that the best fairy godmothers would take over. Literally, the Bests! Luciana stepped up. So did Raine. And even Zahara. We promised your mother everything would work out perfectly.

We still believed in her.

We just thought she was in over her head.

But your mother refused to give up! She insisted she could finish the job, that she was devoted to her princess and knew what she was doing, that they had become friends. And when we told her no, that enough was enough, your mother did something unforgivable.

She made an illegal combination of black and red sparkles to make the princess forget who she was. And then she hid the princess away from family and friends and the fairy godmother world. She would not tell us where she was. When we demanded to know where the princess was, she said, "The princess is fine. I made her happy." And "The story is over."

But of course, the story was just beginning. The whole regular world couldn't help but notice that their perfect princess was gone. And because of that, princesses stopped believing in godmothers and wishes and sparkles.

It was a terrible time.

So the Bests banished her. Not because she failed. Not even because she used those sparkles. The Bests banished her because she did the one thing a fairy godmother should never do.

She put herself before her princess.

In other words: Making the princess happily ever after was her own wish.

Grandmomma looked very sad and a little angry. She looked like someone who wanted to choose her next words very carefully.

"Believe me, I tried. I tried everything I could to make the Bests change their minds. I started the training program. And expanded the Wish List." She took Isabelle's hands. "Isabelle, fairy godmothers are wish granters. Not wish makers. We do not put ourselves first! Ever! This is the reason your sister feels so strongly about following every rule in the book. It's why I can't ask her to help us— because she hasn't been able to forgive your mother for breaking the rules and leaving us.

"At least not yet.

"But I can. And if I can find your mother, I can do even more. I can help the princess. I can offer your mother the chance to apologize. And then I will forgive her. And I bet everyone else will, too." She sighed. "Isabelle, there have been moments when I thought I could find her, but now I have to confess: I need help. I want to see her. I want to be a family again. That's the only way this story can end."

Isabelle sat very quietly for a long time.

"Why do you think I can do this?"

Even though she wanted to help Grandmomma, it was a reasonable question.

"For three reasons," Grandmomma said. "First, because your mother was brave enough to reach out to you." (She meant the ring. And the whisper. And that somehow, Mom knew what Isabelle was up to.) "And, well, you got yourself in hot water, which makes you the perfect person to search for her." She shrugged. "But mostly because you're her daughter. You'll keep my secret. And you happen to be a lot alike—in good ways. Just as she did when she was young, you act with your heart."

Grandmomma held up her wand. "So will you help me?"

Before Isabelle would say yes, she had one more question. "So why the urgency? Why did you have to ruin Level Four? Why couldn't you let me become an official fairy god-mother? Why do you want to find her now?"

A Note to the Reader about the very sad thing you are about to find out:

In every book (and series), even one that is all about happily ever after, there is always a sad part.

For this book, this is it.

Isabelle knew it. She knew the way Grandmomma looked at her. She knew before Grandmomma said it.

But part of her still didn't want to know.

"This is not easy for me to say," Grandmomma said, "but I'm sure you already noticed my hands. And my office."

Grandmomma's hands were thinner than usual. They shook a lot. They didn't look strong. There was also the whole thing with her office. But she was an ancient fairy godmother. Those things were normal.

Or maybe they weren't.

"I haven't wanted to admit it, but it's been clear for a long time: My days as the president of the Fairy Godmother Alliance are limited. Soon, I will not be able to control my wand."

Isabelle ran to her strong, proud, powerful Grandmomma—with the emphasis on *momma*. She was the godmother who had led other godmothers to be great.

She was the godmother who wrote the rules and who had written the book. And now . . .

Even though Grandmomma wasn't a hugger, Isabelle wrapped her arms around her and held on tight.

"Where do I start?" she asked.

Grandmomma reminded her that there was only one rule she had to follow. Isabelle had to do this secretly. Under the sparkle-radar. "Since they think you're going to the Home, they won't worry about you." Then she handed her a wand.

"Was this hers?" Isabelle asked.

"It's newer than that," Grandmomma reminded her. "But I filled it with multicolor sparkles. If I gave you anything else, Luciana and Clotilda might get suspicious."

"So I'm on my own?"

Grandmomma nodded. "Act like a detective. Look for clues. See what you find." It sounded exciting and scary at the same time. "And if you find anything, or suspect any-thing, or need me in any way, just wave that wand in a swirling fashion." She demonstrated what she meant, even though Isabelle was very good at making swirls. "If you do that, I will find you and help you out." She patted Isabelle on the head. "But otherwise, yes. You can't let anyone know what you're doing."

"And you're sure that includes Clotilda?"

"I'm afraid it definitely includes your sister."

As they hugged one more time, Isabelle could feel Grandmomma's heart beat steadily and strongly. Isabelle thought about everything she had told her about Mom.

About her love for her daughters.

And her love for the unhappy princess.

"Isabelle, you can do this," Grandmomma said. "You can find your mom. I believe in you. If you get stuck, ask yourself: What would you do for Nora? And I am sure you'll find your way."

Isabelle wasn't quite so confident. But she wanted to do this more than anything else in the fairy godmother world. "After I find Mom," Isabelle said, "you'll tell

Luciana, Raine, and Kaminari to give me another chance?"

"I will," Grandmomma said.

"And if I don't?"

Grandmomma didn't answer. She didn't have to. There was only one way this story could end.

In other words, Isabelle needed to find Mom quickly.

Chapter Ten

The Very Best Plan to Find Mom

Isabelle climbed out of the basement, ditched her protective gear, walked to her room, and sat on her bed.

She had a lot to think about.

On one hand, Isabelle wanted to twirl and dance. Mom had spoken to her! This hadn't been her imagination. Even though she couldn't tell anyone that the accident hadn't been totally her fault, she finally had a chance to prove herself—with sparkles, and even better, without any of the pesky rules that had been holding her back.

On the other hand, now that she didn't have to follow the

rules, she had no idea what to do. For the first time ever, she could've used some of Clotilda's dos and don'ts—her advice and quick thinking.

She also was sure that this would be a lot easier if she could tell her sister everything.

But Grandmomma had made it clear: Isabelle was on her own. And she couldn't do any magic that would attract attention.

It was a bit overwhelming!

Because she had no idea where to begin, Isabelle went to the one place she always went when she felt scared or lonely or needed a boost of confidence: the top of the tower and the cozy spot between the girlgoyles. For once, their inability to hear and speak was an advantage.

She asked them three questions. "What do you think I should do first?" And "Where do you think Mom is?" And "Do you remember the unhappy princess?"

Obviously, they said nothing.

So she made up their answers, and at the same time, tried to boost her confidence.

"Do what Clotilda would do," one girlgoyle *didn't* say.

The other one silently agreed. "Just leave out the red and black sparkles."

She was sure they remembered the princess as well as Mom—that they'd been friends with her, too. She was sure that they thought she could do this. And that Mom was waiting for her.

And that when this was all done, she would not be living in the Home.

But a sign of some kind would be nice. So she looked up at the sky for the special sparkly star. She started to make the wish she always made, but then she stopped. If she was going to be a great fairy godmother—if she was going to find Mom—she had to start doing and listening and granting. Grandmomma had made it clear: This was her job. So instead of pretending that she could *hope* Mom home, she threw a few sparkles into the sky.

She wondered:

"Where might she be?"

"Why couldn't she help me?"

"What am I going to do first?"

"What *would* I do for Nora?"

Clotilda would say, "Look in the book." But Grandmomma said, "Look in your heart." So that's what she did. And of course, because she couldn't help it, she looked at Mom's ring and held it toward the star.

She expected it to turn green, for responsibility. But instead, the ring sparkled a beautiful light blue, for the power of friendship.

Isabelle couldn't help but feel awful! If she hadn't messed up, she'd probably be with Nora now. She understood why Mom had hidden the princess. She understood what it meant to become friends with a princess. She knew how it felt to be connected not just to the wish, but also to the person who was making it!

And that's when she realized a very important truth: If she wanted to find Mom, she needed to find the unhappy princess.

A plan took shape in Isabelle's mind. If Mom had enough

sparkles to leave her the ring and whisper to her during training, Isabelle was 99.9 percent positive she still had enough sparkles to hear the unhappy princess. And maybe, if Isabelle found the unhappy princess and convinced her to make a wish, Mom would have enough sparkles to appear to grant her wish. And then she would see Isabelle. And together, they would go home.

It was a perfect plan.

It made total sparkly sense.

The only problem was: How was she going to start?

She thought about the picture of the very strong-looking woman—the one who was not the princess, but looked vaguely familiar.

She had to be part of it. Maybe she needed to find her first.

So she sat very still.

And very quietly.

And she thought about the story. About love (yuck) and all the other things the princess must have cared about. She thought about Mom wanting to make her happy. She thought about how hard it would be to have a princess that was unhappy for all this time.

And then she heard something.

It wasn't a whisper—not like the voice during training.

It wasn't a girlgoyle, either.

It was a girl with wild hair and big goals and one gigantic problem.

It was Nora.

Chapter Eleven

Distractions!

Isabelle tried not to listen. She tried not to care.

She knew Nora was not going to help her find the unhappy princess, and that if she wanted to stay under the radar, she had to stay far away from her.

But that was easier said than done.

No matter how hard she tried to focus on the unhappy princess, whoever she was, all she could hear was Nora.

She could hear Nora talking.

She could hear Nora complaining.

She could hear Nora stomping her foot.

She could hear Nora's friends, too, as though they wanted to help her but didn't know how. This made Isabelle feel even worse. Because of her mistakes, Nora probably wasn't going to get help.

That wasn't fair.

It also wasn't right. It wasn't the fairy godmother way.

That's when Isabelle realized something amazing—and somewhat convenient. What was the point of having no rules and a whole wand full of sparkles if you couldn't go visit an old friend? Everyone thought she was at the Home. What was the point of keeping Grandmomma's secret if she couldn't do a little snooping for herself?

If it was really against the rules, Grandmomma would have forbidden it specifically.

With the flick of her wand, Isabelle puffed down to the park where she and Nora first met. Today, the air was chilly. The ground was covered with a crusty layer of snow. Nora stood under a tree with her friends Samantha, Mason, and

Janet. Nearby, a bigger group of kids huddled together. A few others ran around, throwing snowballs or building snow people.

A gust of wind tickled Isabelle's nose.

It looked as if most of the kids were having fun.

But not Nora. When a very tall boy threw a snowball at her (but missed), she shook her fist and yelled, "I'm going to beat you at the ballot box, James Stuart Henderson!"

She did not seem anywhere close to happily ever after. So Isabelle crept closer to hear what Nora was saying.

"Did you hand out the policy sheets?" Nora asked Samantha, breaking through the top layer of snow with her foot. "Did you tell them to pay special attention to pages six and ten and fourteen, where I map out my plans for updating the school's science program? About making the park prettier?"

Samantha promised she had.

Nora ducked when another snowball came flying. "Then why is everyone saying they are voting for James?"

Isabelle turned around to check out the crowd of kids

talking to the tall boy that had thrown the first snowball. They looked as if they were eating treats and having fun. Not talking about serious things like plans and problems and policies.

They also held red, blue, and bright green signs—just like the Grands had during the strike. But these signs were not protests. They said things like: JAMES STUART HENDERSON 4 PREZ. And JAMES STUART HENDERSON IS THE BEST. And VOTE FOR JAMES; GET A SLICE!

In the regular world, unlike in the fairy godmother world, contests and elections were not always fair and square, or in other words, about the issues. Nora didn't seem to know that.

But Samantha, Mason, and Janet did.

"We should order some pizza," Samantha said.

"Or maybe get some candy," Mason suggested.

Janet had the best idea of all. "Or can we get your step-mom to bake?"

Isabelle's mouth watered. Nora's stepmom was an excellent baker, as close to magical as a baker could be in the regular world. Isabelle especially loved the purple macarons she'd made when Isabelle and Nora first became friends. She could practically taste them even now.

But Nora did not want to win that way.

"This shouldn't be a popularity contest, or about free food," she said. "This should be about the issues! And if we are talking issues, I am the only one with a plan for fixing the sidewalk. I am the only one with a plan for adding more crossing guards. And I'm the only one with a plan for raising money with a story night. All of us can come to school in our pajamas. It will be so much fun. My stepmom can make treats for that."

Mason didn't think that was enough. "If you don't want to give out food, maybe help kids with their homework."

"Mason's right," Janet said. "The election is three days away! You have to do something big."

When Nora looked up at the clouds, Isabelle had to stop herself from raising her wand. She could feel Nora wondering how she could make a wish to win the election and still win it the right way—the honorable way. It was just as well that she couldn't figure it out. Isabelle couldn't do anything about it. Not without getting caught.

So even though every muscle in her body wanted to stay, Isabelle had to get out of there. In other words, Isabelle had to find Mom. For herself. And Grandmomma. And Clotilda, too. This was her maximum sparkle responsibility. Isabelle was not going to get any closer to finding her if she stayed here.

So she started walking down the street toward Nora's house and the tree in her backyard. It wasn't as cozy as the spot between the girlgoyles, but it would be cozy enough.

There was only one thing she forgot: Climbing a tree in the winter isn't quite the same as climbing a tree when the weather is warm.

The branches were cold and slippery. There were no leaves to hide in. The ladder was nowhere to be found. So instead of climbing, she sat down on the ground. She examined her ring. (It was now greenish blue.) She took out a notebook and wrote down everything she knew about the unhappy princess before she became unhappy.

Then she drew a few curlicues.

And a few wands and crowns.

All this drawing did not solve her problem. But it did give her an amazing idea—one she should have thought up already!

She had to start at the beginning of the story, to the place where it all began. In other words, the unhappy princess's palace.

Isabelle jumped up and whipped out her wand. She swished it across the horizon.

She needed to go to the scene of the crime—to the unhappy princess's *Once Upon a Time*. To the place where it all began.

Chapter Twelve

The Scene of the Crime

$\mathcal{A}$ moment later, Isabelle stood inside the unhappy princess's castle. Just like Grandmomma's castle, it had a beautiful foyer filled with golden urns and beautiful fountains, and chocolate treats were on every table. There were gigantic towers with gargoyles that did not look like girls, and lions on every door. And there were beautiful rooms filled with flowers and fountains and fancy furniture, most of them covered in gold or silver.

As she snooped around the halls, she saw paintings of

generations of princesses, kings, and queens—all in fancy golden frames.

This was exciting! There would surely be a portrait of the princess hanging on one of these walls.

But after searching every hall, Isabelle gave up. It was clear that when the unhappy princess disappeared (with the help of Mom), her parents were so distraught that they took down her portrait—so Isabelle couldn't see what she looked like.

This was discouraging.

But Isabelle didn't give up.

She decided to go snoop on the current princess, the Cousin of the unhappy one. Maybe that would work.

From the Wish List, she knew that this princess had been on the top of a lot of godmothers' Best Princess lists. (In other words, she'd seemed easy to make happily ever after.) That was because this princess, like the unhappy princess, was also strong and very beloved. She had many useful skills, from math to fine arts to baking, helping animals, and especially making every single person she met feel happy. (In other words, she was good at everything.)

But Isabelle also knew that this princess already had a fairy godmother—an old, cautious one. And she was hovering nearby, waiting for the princess to make a wish! So she had to be careful.

Luckily, the new princess did not have wishing on the brain. Today, she was getting ready to visit sick children in the hospital. She had a bunch of stuffed bunnies to give them to make them feel comforted.

Isabelle thought about Nora and the election. Maybe James was right. Maybe it wasn't wrong for people to hand out snacks. Even though Nora's ideas were excellent, she didn't always have to lecture. Maybe she could listen more. Or have more fun.

As she wondered whether Nora would ever take this advice, Isabelle watched the old godmother. She watched the way she held her wand like a pencil. And how she smiled at the princess like a mother. And how she didn't seem to mind waiting.

And waiting.

And waiting.

Isabelle had to face the facts: This was a dead end. The unhappy princess was definitely not here.

Even more obvious, there was no way that Mom could have left her clues. She wasn't going to magically point her in the right direction or send her a sign or even show up.

It was time to try something else—to visit the castles and lands that the unhappy princess had visited when she was happy, but where her classmates wouldn't be. She couldn't be sure if they would keep her secret.

She visited an ancient castle made of stone, built on the edge of a cliff, and now completely empty.

She visited a Middle Eastern castle, where people now prayed. And she visited the most famous castle of all— Buckingham Palace. She watched the guards with big bearskin hats stand at the door. She tried to make them smile (without magic). But they were good. They didn't even blink.

It was fun. All these places were interesting, but none of them got her any closer to Mom.

Also, no matter how interesting the castle, she could still hear Nora. Complaining. Bossing her friends around. Sighing and putting herself down when she thought no one could hear her.

This was too much.

If Mom had really wanted to help her, she should have whispered more loudly. Or maybe she should have shouted. Or maybe she should have put Isabelle and Clotilda and the fairy godmother world before her unhappy princess!

Maybe Clotilda was right.

Maybe she should forget about Mom.

She had forgotten about *them*. Right?

Chapter Thirteen

Pep Talk Plus Pity Party

When Isabelle was feeling this low and confused, there was only one godmother she could talk to. She was the god-mother who didn't mind breaking a few rules. She was the godmother who could keep a secret from the Bests. She was the godmother who wouldn't judge her.

No surprise. It was Minerva.

Isabelle opened her Wish List to look at the entry on Minerva's princess. Her ancient friend was busy making the great-great-great-great-granddaughter of her very first princess happily ever after. From the very first level of training, Minerva had made it clear that she was loyal to her first princess's family and was going to dedicate her life to making this young girl happy.

Isabelle raised her wand and flicked it three times. She hoped she'd have time for an interruption.

She did. Minerva loved gossip.

"What are you doing here?" Minerva asked. "We were told you were sent straight to the Home."

Isabelle knew Grandmomma didn't want her to spill the beans. But she had already broken one rule (to visit Nora). Also, she knew she was getting nowhere quickly. Minerva was very wise and would probably have a better idea about what she should do.

So she told her everything.

She told her about the voice and Grandmomma being tired and the true story of the unhappy princess—even though it obviously proved that Mom really was the worst fairy godmother ever, or at least pretty bad.

Minerva, however, surprised Isabelle. She understood why Mom did what she did. (In Level Two, she put her princess's wishes above the rules.) "So that's why they got rid of her," Minerva said. "But at least you know she's still out there."

Isabelle agreed. "I'm 99.9 percent sure that Mom can still hear the princess, wherever she may be, and that if she wishes, Mom will appear, and I will talk to her and take her home."

"That's a great idea in theory," Minerva said. "But in reality, it's not going to be easy! Your grandmomma was right about your mom. She was a powerful fairy godmother with stronger magic than anyone else I ever saw. That princess could be anywhere! Even right here!"

Isabelle frowned. This was not the pity party she needed. "What would you do, if you were me?"

Minerva thought about that. "Because the connection between you and your mother is very strong, I would definitely pay attention to everything you see or especially hear."

Paying attention was just another word for doing nothing. And waiting. Isabelle sulked. "You mean, just sit here and wait for a whisper?"

"No." Minerva shook her head. "You have to do something—something that will make her whisper."

Isabelle knew what she meant. "You mean I should get into trouble?"

Minerva thought it was the only way. "If you haven't noticed, the regular world is huge. Your mom had sparkles of immense power." She twirled her wand between her wrinkly fingers. "I assume your grandmomma is not going to give you unlimited sparkles."

"Probably not," Isabelle said. "Do you have any to spare?"

Minerva did not offer any of hers. Just more advice. "Have you heard anything odd lately?"

Isabelle shook her head. "Nothing." Then she added, "Unless you count Nora bossing around her friends."

Minerva smiled. "What's up with her?"

Isabelle paced around the room. "Oh, the usual. Saving the world. Running for class president. Getting on every-one's nerves."

Minerva laughed. She understood.

"I want to help her, but I can't get distracted," Isabelle said. She told Minerva about the election. "Samantha is doing her best to be a good friend, but it's not going well." She was feeling worse by the second. "I wish I hadn't read that old book. I wish I had studied, like Angelica and Fawn. I wish I still had that Number One pin!" She asked, "Do you know what they're doing?"

Minerva whipped out a snow globe. "Of course I do." (She was the nosiest fairy godmother ever!) "I made this after I got a look at your grandmomma's spyglass." She shook it hard. "In it, we can see everyone. Maybe it will give you some ideas!"

Isabelle loved snow globes. "Can I try?"

She shook it hard. There was Angelica in South America with Luciana. They were working hard to save the rain forest with an activist princess.

Isabelle shook the snow globe again so she could see Fawn.

She was in Japan helping a princess prepare for a big speech. Minerva knew all about it. "She helped her princess secure a spot on the boys' soccer team and organize a march for women's rights!"

When Isabelle sulked, Minerva told Isabelle to snap out of it. "I also heard your sister is about to be named Number Three."

"She is?"

Minerva held out her hand for the snow globe. "Roxanne is officially happily ever after."

Isabelle stared at the magic toy. She asked, "Do you think Clotilda will forgive Mom?" Although there were times when Isabelle wished she could remember anything about Mom (Isabelle was a tiny baby when she went away), she also knew that it might hurt more to have memories.

She remembered hugging her. And talking to her. And watching her do magic.

She remembered being left behind.

"Your sister is very smart," Minerva said. "Like your mom, she is also proud and, no offense, a little stuffier than she needs to be."

Isabelle nodded. "No offense taken!"

"But you don't get to be a Best without having a huge heart. So this is what I think: There is only one thing your sister won't forgive, and that's not trying. Especially when you have the opportunity to do something great."

Isabelle agreed. Even though she'd like to congratulate her sister right now—even though she'd like to sit with her between the girlgoyles—she knew she had a bigger job.

She shook the snow globe. Then she shook it again. And again. Maybe she could find her mom this way.

But all she saw was fog. Light-blue fog. It was coming from her ring. The hint of green was gone.

"Did you hear her?" Minerva asked.

Isabelle sighed. "Nope. All I ever hear is Nora," she said. "Right now, she's talking to her stepmom."

Minerva asked, "Do you have any other clues to go on?"

Isabelle reminded her about the sparkles and the picture of the mysterious woman who was not the unhappy princess. "That's all I have." She shook her head. "But I don't think I can concentrate on anything when Nora needs me."

Minerva put her hands on Isabelle's shoulders and looked her straight in the eyes. "Then I think you'd better go help her. Get it out of your system."

This was probably bad advice, but it was the bad advice Isabelle wanted to hear. "You don't think I'll get in trouble?"

"Of course I think you'll get in trouble," Minerva said, bursting into laughter, "if you get caught."

Isabelle knew this was true. "Can you help me?"

Minerva shook the snow globe one last time. "I might be able to create a small sparkly distraction."

"Another strike?"

Minerva shook her head. "I was thinking more like snow. A whole bunch of it." She smiled. "But I can't keep it up for long. Probably just until the magic hour." (In other words: midnight.)

It would have to be enough.

"Thanks, Minerva," Isabelle said. "No matter what Grandmomma says, you're the best!"

She didn't waste a second. She flicked her wand and went back to Nora's house. By now Nora would be there.

Isabelle knew it was a risk, but she had to see whether she could help her.

Chapter Fourteen

More Serious Than Ever Before

When Isabelle arrived outside Nora's house, the snow was already coming down hard. The streets were empty. Isabelle stuck out her tongue and ate a few flakes. (Peppermint flakes were better, but these were tasty, too.)

First, she checked to see whether any other godmothers were lurking around.

When she was sure she was the only magical person nearby, she knocked on the door. To her delight, Gregory answered. He was Nora's little brother. She wasn't sure how well Rule Three C worked on him because he was a boy. But since he was really young the last time they saw each other, it didn't matter. He didn't recognize her.

"Are you here to help Nora win?" he asked. "Or do you want to make snow angels with me?"

Snow angels sounded like a lot of fun, but then a huge gust of wind swooped by. Isabelle shivered. "I'm here to help Nora. But maybe we can make them tomorrow."

"That's what everybody always says!" Gregory said, opening the door wider so she could come inside and look around.

Nora's house was covered in decorations like candles and blue streamers, and it smelled amazing. "What is your mom making?" Isabelle asked.

"Latkes," Gregory said. "Three different kinds. One with carrots and zucchini. One with jalapeño peppers. And the classic—fried potato, served with applesauce and sour cream."

Isabelle couldn't wait to try them!

"Mom is also making chocolate ice cream out of snow!"

Gregory added. "And doughnuts, too. With chocolate sauce for dipping."

Chocolate ice cream! And doughnuts with dipping sauce. That woman was a magician! Isabelle forgot to be cautious and ran into the kitchen to introduce herself again to Nora and her stepmom, and hopefully grab a plate.

Nora was sitting at the table, drawing a poster. "Do I know you?" she asked.

"We were in the same class last year," Isabelle said, talking quickly so Nora couldn't ask too many questions. "I wanted to come by and help with your campaign because I think you'll be the best president." She smiled and flicked a blue sparkle toward her hand to help win Nora over. "Way better than James."

The sparkle must have worked, or maybe Nora was simply facing the facts. All this snow meant that her friends were stuck at home. School might be canceled. She didn't have the luxury of wondering too much about why Isabelle was here.

In other words, they got to work. "Are you good with lettering?" Nora asked. "I really need some nice signs. And maybe a few catchy slogans. And something else that James can't make."

Isabelle flinched. That sounded a lot like a wish. Luckily, no fairy godmother showed up to ruin the moment. "I can definitely make some signs. And also some bracelets!"

"That's an amazing idea," Nora said.

Even though it was dangerous, Isabelle showed her the bracelet Nora had given her in Level Three. "I could make one like this." Then she had a great idea. "Or we could decorate them with glitter."

Nora's stepmom clapped her hands. "I love glitter," she said. "My sister and I used to play with it all the time."

Of course, Isabelle remembered Auntie Viv. She loved glitter so much that Isabelle had thought she might be magical!

But she couldn't say that. So she said, "It makes everyone feel happy. It might even earn you some votes."

Nora didn't totally agree (or remember giving her the

bracelet), but since she was outnumbered and in no position to argue, she made room for Isabelle and showed her the posters she had made so far. There were two.

The first said: TEN REASONS TO VOTE FOR NORA. The other said: TEN REASONS NOT TO VOTE FOR JAMES.

That didn't seem very nice.

"You think it's that bad?" Nora asked, seeing her expression.

Isabelle had to admit it was bad.

Nora was stuck. "But I don't know what else to do! James is really popular. He is friends with everyone and plays three sports and has a great sense of humor. And even though he doesn't seem to care about any of the problems in the school, he hands out candy. And pizza. So no matter what I say, everyone is going to vote for him." She tore the posters into pieces. "Even my friends."

So the three of them got to work. They made glittery signs (with a few sparkles secretly thrown in) that said VOTE FOR NORA. And NORA IS AWESOME. And NORA WILL MAKE THE SCHOOL HAPPILY EVER AFTER.

Nora liked that. In fact, with each new project, she seemed to be getting more confident and even happy. So when they were done, they made some bracelets for Samantha, Mason, and Janet to thank them for sticking with her even when she was grumpy.

When they were finished, Nora slumped on the couch. "I wish all of this was over." She was tired of running for president. She admitted she'd been unkind to her friends, but she couldn't stop herself. At the same time, she really wanted to win.

Isabelle made her another bracelet to keep herself from granting that wish. "Your friends will forgive you." She assured Nora that the snow would clear and she'd be able to give her speech.

A very thick stack of papers sat on Nora's desk. "That's it," Nora said. "I think it's really good."

It looked really long. Isabelle picked it up and paged through it. There were a lot of words on every page.

"Maybe we could shorten it?" Isabelle suggested.

Nora's stepmom frowned. "Nora wants her chance to say

everything she believes in. And I support that. Even if she loses, she should present all her ideas. I think that it's hard to be happy when we are not our true selves."

"Thanks," Nora said to her stepmom—and Isabelle. "Even if it is too long and too boring, at least the signs and bracelets will be nice."

When they were done packing up everything for tomorrow, Nora's stepmom handed them plates of latkes with applesauce. She looked out the window. "The snow is really pretty. If school is canceled tomorrow, do you want to come over and snowshoe on the trail?"

Isabelle thought that sounded great. But hiking up the trail sounded like something that might encourage Nora to make a wish. Nora put down her pen. "My dad says that my mom loved that trail. When I'm there, I am sure she can see me."

Her stepmom gave her a huge hug. "Nora, she can always see you. And she is very proud. And so am I."

Isabelle, of course, had those same feelings when it came to her own mom. "What was she like?" she asked.

"I don't really remember," Nora said. "But Dad says she was just like me." She smiled. "So I guess she really cared about a lot of things."

Nora's dad must have been eavesdropping, because he walked in the room. "Your mom was one of the best people I ever met. She was strong and brave and never backed down from an argument—especially when she knew she was right." He gave Nora a squeeze. "But even when she got sick, she believed in magic, too. In happily ever after. She made so many wishes. For herself. And then for you. For your happiness."

Happily ever after? Magic? Wishes?

This couldn't just be a coincidence. (She knew that by now.)

Isabelle leaned forward. "What was she like?"

Nora's dad handed Isabelle a big fat book. It was a photo album, sort of like a Wish List for their family. "After she died, I made this for Nora."

Isabelle opened the book. She saw a picture of Nora as a baby. And Nora as a girl. And then, tucked into a back pocket, was something else. It was a picture of Nora with a woman who looked a lot like the woman in the picture that Grandmomma showed her.

"Was that your mom?"

Nora smiled. "That was her."

Isabelle wanted to get up and twirl! (But she didn't. She held it in.) This was the break she'd been waiting for.

Grandmomma was wrong. The picture that was with Mom's stuff had to be the unhappy princess. She was Nora's mom. It couldn't be any other way!

Isabelle thought about everything she knew about the unhappy princess, trying to make the pieces fit. Nora's mom was good. Everyone loved her. She believed in wishes, even after she got sick. That's why Mom needed the healing sparkles.

She stuffed down one more latke. "I have to go," she said, pointing to the wall clock. It was almost the magic hour.

Nora looked out the window. "So, do you want to come over tomorrow?"

"If it's still snowing, absolutely," Isabelle said, even though she knew the snow would be gone by then. And maybe, if her hunch was right and Nora's mom had been the unhappy princess, her mom would be cleared and Isabelle could be back in training and she would be able to help Nora.

At least that's what she hoped would happen.

She went outside and whipped out her wand to make the swirly move, the one Grandmomma had called "their signal."

She waited for Grandmomma to appear. To help her figure this out.

But Grandmomma did not appear.

Someone else did.

That someone was the one godmother Isabelle didn't want to see.

That someone was her sister. Clotilda.

Chapter Fifteen

Sisters! A Very Short Chapter.

*D*oes it feel as if they've been here before? With Isabelle in trouble and Clotilda walking in to save the day?

There might be a reason for that.

This was not the first time Clotilda had caught her sister breaking rules.

This was not the first time Clotilda had looked annoyed with Isabelle.

This was not the first time Clotilda looked as though she wanted to throw up her hands and say, "For all that is sparkly," or "For pity's sake," or "Who can keep calm and sparkle on when you are breaking all these rules?"

But this was different. This was Isabelle breaking the rules—with the help of someone powerful.

This was Isabelle knowing something that Clotilda didn't.

This was Isabelle in control. "Why aren't you at the Home?" Clotilda asked.

As far as Clotilda was concerned, Isabelle had flunked out of training. She was not supposed to be standing in a fairy godmother–induced snowstorm outside the home of her first practice princess.

"Let me explain," Isabelle said.

First, she apologized. She told Clotilda that she would have told her everything, but that Grandmomma had made her promise not to. And then, because flattery was still the best way to butter up her sister, she told her that she was really proud of her for being named Number Three. And that she would soon be Number One.

And then she told her about the picture.

And Nora's mom.

And everything else, too.

Clotilda looked a bit stunned. "Grandmomma sent you to look for Mom?"

Isabelle knew this sounded ludicrous. "She wants to forgive her. And bring her back to the fairy godmother world." She hoped Clotilda wouldn't be mad.

"So you won't tell Luciana what I'm doing?"

Clotilda put down her wand. "Of course not." Clotilda put her dainty hand on Isabelle's shoulder. "She was my mom, too. I miss her. Every day."

This was the truth they'd always known but never really talked about. Even though they were different. Even though they did not do things the same way and were good at different things. They were sisters.

And that meant that, just as Isabelle wanted Clotilda to do well, Clotilda wanted Isabelle to do well. It meant that she missed Mom just as much as Isabelle did.

"So if you didn't know what I was doing, why are you here?" Isabelle asked. "How did you find me?"

"Because Grandmomma told me where you were. Because she needs you. Now."

"What do you mean, she needs me now?" Isabelle asked.

Clotilda said, "You need to come home." She held out her hand so Isabelle could grab it. "Hold on tight."

Chapter Sixteen

A Chapter with a Whole Lot of Mothers!

It doesn't matter whether you live in the fairy godmother world or the regular world. Seeing your grandmomma sick in bed is scary.

Isabelle ran to Grandmomma's side. She held her hand.

Grandmomma looked tired and weak. But her eyes still looked bright. "What did you find out?" she asked Isabelle.

Isabelle told her what Nora's dad said. "Her real mom believed in happily ever after. Her real mom made wishes." She squeezed Grandmomma's hand. "I think Nora's mom was the unhappy princess. I think Mom wanted those aquamarine sparkles to heal her, but she was too late."

Isabelle showed Clotilda the picture of Nora's mom.

Clotilda shook her head. Grandmomma wasn't convinced. She said, "The regular world is full of people who believe in happily ever after and are not the unhappy princess."

Even more important: If Nora's mom was the unhappy princess, then what had Mom been doing all this time?

Isabelle was so frustrated. She had been so sure! "I felt as if I was close. All the pieces fit. I even wondered whether that's why I got Nora to begin with." (Because of the *no coincidences* thing.)

Grandmomma sighed. "I wish I could tell you that your hunch was correct. But I can assure you, I was not mistaken. The unhappy princess was a real-life royal princess." She took a deep breath. Her skin looked pale. "Also, Isabelle, when I match princesses with trainees, I don't rely on hunches. I rely on experience and other measurable data. Nora might have seemed like an unusual choice to you, but trust me, she really wasn't. She was independent like you. She had a big heart like you. And also like you, she was a girl who missed her real mom."

This made sense.

But it was also a disappointment.

Isabelle had so wanted to be right. And not just for herself—for Nora, too.

When she was at Nora's house, she felt happy, too. And that wasn't just because of Nora. It was also because of Gregory, Samantha, Mason, and Janet. It was because of Nora's dad and stepmom. Isabelle said, "Her dad is as kind as any king. Her stepmom is the nicest, kindest, most wonderful person I have ever met. She bakes magical treats, almost as good as ours. And she even likes sparkles— or what she calls glitter."

Grandmomma smiled. So did Clotilda. Grandmomma said, "She seems like a nice lady." In other words, she was also pretty sure that Isabelle was no closer to finding Mom than she'd been when she started.

Isabelle needed to start all over again. But first she had a favor to ask. "Please, can I help Nora just a little bit? She's going to lose that election big-time. And all her friends in the process. I don't want her to be alone."

Grandmomma looked at Clotilda. "What do you think?" (In other words, could they keep this from the Bests?)

Clotilda wasn't sure. "Just to be clear, you're asking us to break the rules?"

Isabelle nodded. "Not all the rules. Just look the other way and don't tell anyone you know what I'm up to."

"And do you think you can find Mom when you're done?" Clotilda asked.

Isabelle held Grandmomma's hand tighter than ever. "All I'm sure of is that Nora needs me."

Grandmomma smiled. That was because Isabelle was acting like an official fairy godmother. She nodded to Clotilda. "What can we whip up so she doesn't get caught?"

Clotilda smiled. "How about a touch of fog?"

For the first time in what felt like forever, Isabelle twirled. "The second I figure out anything, I'll give you the signal."

When Isabelle got back to Nora's, it was morning. The snow had melted, but a thick blanket of fog covered her neighborhood.

Isabelle banged on Nora's door.

Her stepmom answered, balancing a plate of cinnamon rolls with icing in her hand. "You're back! I'm so glad!" She offered her a roll. "How are you, Isabelle? Nora just went to school. I'm making treats for her big speech. These are ooey gooey cinnamon rolls laced with chocolate ribbons."

Ribbons of chocolate reminded her of her sister. "They sound great," Isabelle said, her tummy already growling. "Are you making anything else?"

"Purple macarons. And whoopie pies."

Maybe it was the way she smiled. Or said, "You're back!" Or maybe it was because she was making all of Isabelle's favorite fairy godmother treats. Or maybe it was because she was wearing a ring. And not just any ring. She was wearing Nora's ring.

And it was shining bright, like the entire prism of light.

Isabelle knew that she shouldn't rely on hunches. But every bone in her body was telling her that this time, she was right.

"What do you remember about the story of the unhappy princess?" she asked, grabbing a cinnamon roll and taking a bite.

"The unhappy princess?" Nora's stepmom looked puzzled.

Isabelle told her to sit down, that this was important. "You know, the princess who never got what she wanted, the princess who disappeared, that made everyone stop believing in wishes." When Nora's stepmom still didn't answer, Isabelle pointed to her hand. "Where did you get that ring?"

"It's my ring. I've always had it," Nora's stepmom said. She looked a little annoyed. "I don't really have time for fairy tales right now. Nora's counting on me to bring snacks for her big speech. Will you help me pack these up?"

But Isabelle wasn't going to let her go anywhere. "I think we both know that the story of the unhappy princess isn't just a fairy tale." Isabelle put her hand on Nora's stepmom's arm. "Please, tell me what you know. Please?"

Unfortunately, she didn't know much.

The Story of the Unhappy Princess, as
Told by Nora's Stepmom
When I was young, there was a princess. She seemed very kind and beautiful, but also, most unhappy.
So she gave up her crown.
I don't really know more than that.

"What do you mean, you don't know more than that?" Isabelle cried.

Nora's stepmom shrugged. "To be honest, I don't really worry about princesses all that much. But what I *can* tell you is that I believe in magic. Right after she disappeared, I met Nora's dad and Nora, and they were so unhappy. Almost right away, I knew they needed me. I knew we could be a happy family. More than that, for the first time, *I* was happy—happier than I had ever been before."

Isabelle grabbed Nora's stepmom's hands. "Before you met Nora's dad, by any chance, did you make a wish?" She knew that sounded odd, so she added, "Since you said you believe in magic."

Nora's stepmom looked funny. "I used to make wishes all the time, although lately, I haven't." She smiled. "The truth is, I haven't had to. I have everything I want."

Isabelle started jumping up and down. "Well, can you make one now? For Nora. Or for yourself. Or for me to stop talking. Anything! Make a wish. If you do, I believe that a fairy godmother will appear. She will come and grant your wish, just as she did when you wished to be happy and met Nora's dad."

This had become more than awkward, but Isabelle had more than a little hunch about what was about to happen.

"What would make you happily ever after right now?" she asked. (She hoped it wasn't a wish for more wishes.)

Nora's stepmom's eyes turned bright, as if she were remembering something important. "I know."

Without wasting another second, Nora's stepmom closed her eyes. She held her ring to her heart. As she felt her heart, she remembered another day. Another wish. An old friend.

She made a wish.

It wasn't a grand wish. She had never been that kind of princess. But just like the best wishes in history, it came straight from her heart.

I bet you know what happened next. First, a lot of multicolor sparkles filled the air.

Then some bright light.

Then a few more sparkles (but this time mostly blue).

And then a woman.

She had long, wild hair that fell loose below her shoulders. Her smile was big, and she wore a hat with a pom-pom on the top. She wore jeans with sparkly hearts down the side. And a T-shirt that said (in glitter) THE WORLD NEEDS MORE SPARKLES.

Isabelle clapped her hands.

Finally.

Mom.

Chapter Seventeen

What Sparkles Can Do

Many things can happen when someone finds out that they have a real fairy godmother.

They can feel joy.

They can feel comfort.

But the magic of sparkles can do much more than that. Sparkles can heal a broken heart. They can bring a family together. Or in the case of Nora's stepmom, they can make one.

Or maybe even two.

First thing first, Mom checked in with her princess, because she looked positively shocked. "Hi, Hannah," she said. Then because of (stupid) Rule Three C, she reintroduced herself. Probably for the umpteenth time.

When she said, "I am your fairy godmother," Nora's mom almost fell over.

She pinched herself to make sure she wasn't dreaming. "Isabelle was right? You're here to grant my wish?"

Isabelle twirled five-and-a-half times. She waited for Mom to grant it—but Mom had more pressing things to do first, things that she'd been wanting to do for a very long time.

First, she introduced herself to Isabelle. And then she gave her the kind of big, long hug that only mothers can give.

There was so much to say. (And a wish to grant!) But before anyone could say or do anything, Grandmomma and Clotilda appeared in a brilliant flash of light.

Clotilda raised her wand to meet Isabelle's. (That was a first!) She said, "Isabelle! You did it!"

"Victoria," Grandmomma said. "I've missed you so much. I'm so happy to see you."

First, Mom bowed her head to Grandmomma. And then to Clotilda. Then she twirled in a circle and hugged them both so long and tightly that they had to ask her to let go. "Mom. You did it. You repaired the fairy godmother world. And, Tildy! Look at you! I'm so proud. You are everything I always wanted to become—everything I hoped you would be."

And then she turned to Isabelle.

Isabelle hoped she wasn't going to say something about how she'd grown. Or how proud she was. Or some excuse for being gone.

Mom had something more important to say. "Isabelle. Clotilda. Will you please forgive me?"

"Can you?" Grandmomma asked them both.

Isabelle wanted to say yes, but first, there was one thing she had to know. "When you were gone, why didn't you try harder to see us? It's the only thing that doesn't make sense."

Before Mom could say anything, Grandmomma raised her wand. (That meant she was going to say something important.) "Isabelle and Clotilda, when your mother was banished, the Bests didn't know what to do with you. They knew your mother would want to see you. They even worried that you were too much like her—that you would ultimately break the rules. Plus, they wanted to know where your mother had stashed that unhappy princess! So, after much debate, they decided to send you both to the Home. For good."

Clotilda said, "They wanted to take away our sparkle?"

Mom said, "Even when I promised that the princess was happy, they wouldn't believe me. They didn't understand."

Grandmomma said, "So I pleaded with the Bests to let me offer a compromise. I promised your mother that I would raise you both in the fairy godmother world, as long as your mother stayed away and never tried to contact you." She held out her hands for Isabelle and Clotilda. "Under the circumstances, it was the best choice."

Mom apologized again. "That's why I stayed away. For you. For your happiness."

Grandmomma said, "Because she loves you." She looked at her daughter. "Over the years, I tried to find you. I hoped you could see them. But my hopes were only suspicions until now."

When everyone was done congratulating and forgiving each other, Mom got serious. "Thank you for taking care of them. I am ready to come home. But will anyone believe me? Will everyone accept that the unhappy princess was never unhappily ever after?"

Everyone looked at Nora's stepmom.

"Is there something you need me to do?" she asked Mom.

Mom laughed. "Just let me tell them your wish. Not this last one. The first one."

Isabelle said, "Yes, what was her wish?"

"The princess wished to disappear," Mom said. "To find a family. Have a regular life filled with love. And I did it. I made her happily ever after!"

"She actually used the word *disappear*?" Grandmomma looked very remorseful. "I should have believed you'd never make a wish for yourself."

Mom shook her head. "I'd never do that. I learned from you."

Then Grandmomma raised her wand to override Rule Three C so Nora's stepmom could remember all the details, too.

Isabelle could tell when she did, because her face changed. From happy to sad to happy again and then to happily ever after. Then she bowed deeply to all the fairy godmothers.

"Did you really wish to not be a princess? To be Nora's mom?" Isabelle asked.

"I might love wishing," Nora's stepmom said, "but I was never truly suited to all the princess rules."

There were all kinds of important reasons for rules. But nothing was more important than happiness. And nothing made happiness like family.

They each grabbed some treats (Mom had given Hannah a lot of recipes) and caught up.

Grandmomma told Mom what was going on in the fairy godmother world. She told her about training and survival of the sparkliest and all twelve editions, as well as the changes they'd made, especially in the last few seasons.

Mom told them about the challenges in the regular world—how girls didn't always have equal rights or opportunities, but that in the last few seasons, that was changing, too.

They all agreed that fairy godmothers still had a ton of work to do. "I'm so glad that you understand that all girls are princesses—that everyone deserves happily ever after. And that it looks different to everyone."

Then she asked Grandmomma if she could borrow her wand. She had a wish to grant.

Of course Grandmomma said yes.

But as the room filled with light blue sparkles, Isabelle pointed to the clock.

"Nora's about to take the stage!"

Hannah gasped. "My treats!"

"I'll get us to the school," Clotilda said. "Easy peasy lemon squeezy!"

Chapter Eighteen

So Close to H.E.A. We Can Taste It

*L*ickety-split, they flew to the school. (Not literally, of course. But as fast as sparkles could get them.)

They were just in time, too.

Nora stood on the stage. When she saw Isabelle, her stepmom, and a whole bunch of other ladies in very loud clothes and somewhat overdressed, she couldn't help but wave. And smile.

Then she tested the microphone. She held her big long speech in her hands.

"Friends, this is what I was going to read to you today.

But a few minutes ago, I had a new idea. It is such a great idea, it's almost magical."

Samantha stood up and started clapping. (Probably because the old speech was so long.)

"This week, talking to all of you, I realized that to be a great president of the class, you need three things. You need to be kind—to others and also to yourself. So that we can understand each other. We need to work together so we can help each other be as happy as possible." Nora paused and smiled. "I learned that from my stepmom."

When the crowd stopped clapping, she continued. "I also realized that being a president requires commitment and determination. This is because problems are complicated. They're going to take lots of creativity and hard work to solve." She looked at James. "If you vote for James, I'm still going to help solve those problems."

And then she waved to Isabelle. "And you need friendship. And enthusiasm. And confidence." She held her hand up as if she were waving a wand. "I call that gusto."

When her friends were sure she was done speaking, they all clapped. But Nora wasn't done. "During this campaign, I have learned that James and I have a lot in common—in fact, all of us do. I have learned that we can all be trusted to do a good job. I believe that all people are ready and willing to make our world better." She took a deep breath. "If you do, too, vote for me. Or James. I have a feeling, whoever wins, we are going to change the school together."

Then she sat down.

But everyone else stood up.

And then they got in line to vote.

You might think that Nora won that election. That her stepmom wished for her to win.

But sadly, she did not. She lost by five votes.

So it had nothing to do with magic when the students lobbied for a second vote. For copresident. Nora won that by a landslide.

Chapter Nineteen

Extravaganza Time

It's probably been pretty obvious for a while that this story is going to end with happily ever after. It *is* a story about fairy godmothers. When you think about it, there was no other way to end it.

When Isabelle, Clotilda, Mom, and Grandmomma returned to the fairy godmother world, the Bests acted a tad timid, but when Mom and Grandmomma assured them that the unhappy princess could not be happier, they welcomed her home with open arms. The truth was, Grandmomma was right about a lot of things, but especially that fairy godmothers didn't hold a grudge. They were happy to welcome Mom into the fairy godmother world again—and Mom was happy to be back.

This meant only one thing: an Extravaganza!

Without further ado, the Bests prepared an amazing feast. They decorated the castle like a victory celebration, with streamers, popcorn garlands, and balloons. They covered the tables with noisemakers and, of course, trays of delicious snacks. To Isabelle's delight, they told everyone to dress casually. No uncomfortable dresses required!

Even Grandmomma had to admit that fashion didn't have to hurt. "Sometimes, the best shoes in the world are a pair of fuzzy slippers."

She also prepared an extra-special surprise for Mom. "I found some old girlgoyles in the basement," Grandmomma said. "I remember how you used to love talking to those girls up in the tower."

"Wait a minute," Isabelle said. "The girlgoyles can talk?"

Grandmomma, Clotilda, and Mom stared at Isabelle. "You didn't know?" Clotilda chuckled a little bit. "If you give them a little sparkle, they will keep you up all night."

But Mom looked upset. "You got the ring. Did you not see the blue sparkles? They should have worked like a charm!" She began to apologize again. "Maybe I should stay here with Isabelle. I don't need to see everyone at once. Instead, I can help her talk to the girlgoyles."

Grandmomma knew her daughter was getting nervous. The party was a chance for Mom to see everyone, reintroduce herself, and return to the fairy godmother world. "No one is angry anymore. They all want to forgive you. Isabelle can figure out how to talk to the girlgoyles later."

"It wasn't your fault," Isabelle said, still shocked that all this time, the girlgoyles could talk. "I did find those sparkles. I even put them in the girlgoyles' hands. But I must have used them incorrectly. Because they didn't work." She added, "You have to go to the Extravaganza. I'll wait up, if you want to sit in the tower tonight." (She didn't expect to go herself, since she had not passed training officially.)

But Grandmomma had one more surprise up her sleeve. She'd learned as much from Isabelle as Isabelle had learned from her. "It seems to me that some rules are meant to be smashed to smithereens," she said.

Mom nodded. "In other words, we can all talk to the girl-goyles later. You're coming with us."

Isabelle stood still so Clotilda could make her a cool outfit, including jeans, a bomber jacket covered in sequins, and a hat just like mom's silver-and-blue cloche.

Now they were ready. "To the castle we go!" Isabelle said.

When they arrived, everyone wanted to welcome Mom home. Like the Bests, they also wanted to apologize. And they wanted Mom to share what she'd learned.

But Isabelle wanted to introduce her to her friends first.

She grabbed Angelica and Fawn. "Mom, meet the future Bests."

Her friends bowed their heads. "So sparkly to meet you," they said at the exact same time.

They also apologized to Isabelle for not believing her story about the old rule book, and for Angelica's version of the unhappy princess story. "We're so glad you both are here. We always knew those rumors couldn't be true."

Next were the Grands, especially Minerva. "You don't know how happy I am to see justice served," Minerva said.

"I never understood why they called you the Worsts," Mom said.

Next, they danced. They played party games. They talked to every fairy godmother in the room.

When it was time for dinner, Grandmomma took the podium. "Before we eat, I have some announcements to make. The first is the easiest. I would like to congratulate Angelica, Fawn, and our friends the Grands for their exceptional four levels of godmother training. They are officially official. And I couldn't be more delighted."

She pointed her wand toward the wall to reveal the HAPPILY EVER AFTER: THE LAST LINE OF EVERY GREAT STORY plaque.

"You fixed it!" Isabelle said. Everyone clapped politely. (They knew there was more. Grandmomma was only getting started.) "Did it take strong sparkles to fix?"

"No sparkles at all," Grandmomma said, frowning just a tad. (Remember: Fairy godmothers did not believe in using sparkles for mundane projects.) "All I needed was a little bit of glue."

When everyone was done applauding the new sign, Grandmomma had one more godmother to thank. "I also want to honor my granddaughter Isabelle. All by herself, she took on a big challenge. She acted as bravely and kindly as any godmother could."

At this point, Minerva stood up. She had a sign of her own. So did Angelica, Fawn, Irene, and MaryEllen. Their signs all said the same thing: MAKE ISABELLE OFFICIAL.

"She made that gnarly tree!" Angelica said.

"She helped end the strike!" Fawn said.

"And she made her princess happy without ever really reading one ounce of fine print!" Minerva said.

"What do you say, Isabelle?" Grandmomma winked at

her. "Are you ready to join your class? Do you believe in yourself? Do you trust yourself to be a great fairy godmother?" She held up the Number One pin (hopefully still with the secret sparkles inside). "Do you want this back? Or not?"

Isabelle walked slowly to the podium.

She walked slowly because she had a lot to consider.

Did she trust herself?

A lot of people were counting on her.

And there was also that wish.

Isabelle took the pin. She smiled at Minerva, Angelica, Fawn, Irene, MaryEllen, Zahara, and most of all, Mom and Clotilda.

"A wish is more than a pact between a godmother and a princess. A wish is a promise. A wish is hope. A wish is what we do to make the world better." She took a deep breath. "Earlier today, Nora's stepmom made the best wish ever— for me to be Nora's fairy godmother and lifelong friend." She hugged her Grandmomma. "So yes, I want to be official. I believe I can make Nora happy. But I also know that a girl like Nora is going to have a lot of complicated wishes. And I still have a lot to learn. So can official fairy godmothers still go back to training? And for pity's sake, can we please get rid of Rule Three C?"

The crowd went crazy. (The truth was that no one liked Three C.)

Grandmomma could barely speak. "Yes, let's get rid of Rule Three C. Let's never speak of it again!"

Now the godmothers wanted to sparkle on, but Grandmomma had one more announcement to make. "Mothers, I have one final thing to say. I am stepping down. I will no longer be the president of the Fairy Godmother Alliance. I will no longer run training. And I do not want to ever edit another book!"

Everyone laughed. This was a job that very few godmothers wanted to do.

"I am officially handing in my wand. And my sparkles. I welcome any of you to the castle. But for me, there will be no more magic. I want to enjoy time with my family."

Luciana joined Grandmomma at the podium. "You can imagine that I have some work to do. Following in Elizabeth Marie's footsteps is virtually impossible.

"So this is what we're going to do. I am stepping down from active service. From now on, I will run training."

Luciana continued. "Kaminari has offered to take over the presidency. She has also agreed to edit the book with the help of Victoria, who has graciously offered to share her new knowledge of the regular world and princesses of all sorts. This means that we have a new top three. Raine is Number One, Clotilda is Number Two, and Minerva is Number Three."

Minerva looked almost as surprised as everyone else in the room. "I am?"

Grandmomma said, "You are." She shook the ancient godmother's hand. "I think it will be a good thing for the Bests to include someone with so much experience."

Minerva looked as if she was about to faint. "As long as no one starts calling me and my pals 'The Olds'!"

Everyone laughed. They cheered for Raine, Clotilda, and Minerva. Isabelle told Luciana she'd see her soon. And then she did what she always did.

She hurried back to her friends, the girlgoyles, this time for a real-live, out-loud chat.

Finally!

Chapter Twenty

The Last Chapter, Plus a Promise

Isabelle climbed to the top of the tower and sat between the girlgoyles. She pulled two perfect sparkles out of her Number One pin.

She gave one to each girlgoyle—right between the claws.

For the first time ever, she didn't mind waiting.

But (thank goodness) these sparkles were fairly fresh. They didn't take long to work.

"Isabelle!" Francoise said.

Bernadette gave Isabelle a stony hug. "We've been waiting a long time to talk to you."

Isabelle laughed. "I didn't know."

"We kept waiting for you to figure it out," Francoise said. "There were so many things you could have avoided if you had just talked to us."

This was technically true. But some lessons are best learned on their own.

Especially when they involve fine print. Or choices. Or footnotes. Or magic.

Isabelle told them about Nora and Samantha and how she found Mom. (But they already knew. All this time, they couldn't speak, but they could hear.)

And they told her about her mom as a girl. "She used to talk to us all the time," Bernadette said. Francoise added, "And we used to help her study."

This was news to Isabelle. "Could you do that for me? Maybe help me read the fine print?"

"Absolutely," Francoise said.

Bernadette snapped her fingers and whipped out a magnifying glass. "What else are we here for?"

Now Isabelle couldn't help it. She stood up and twirled. She hugged the girlgoyles. And she almost cried.

Isabelle was sure she was going to be a great fairy godmother—maybe even as great as her sister (but probably not). In fact, she couldn't wait until tomorrow so she could go check in with Nora without having to reintroduce herself. She knew Nora was going to need some time to find the right wish—the perfect wish—the one that would help her change the world (and be happily ever after).

In the meantime, she knew they were going to have all kinds of adventures together.

That was because they were both

a. kind, determined, and full of gusto.

b. focused on making a better world. (And having a blast!)

c. ready for anything!

In the end (and this is that), this was what Isabelle had always wanted. To be a great fairy godmother. To the best princess ever.

In other words: happily ever after.

All of the above.

The End

Acknowledgments

Dear Readers,

At the end of each of the previous Wish List books, I have had the privilege to thank my family and friends, as well as my agent, Sarah Davies, and the great people at Scholastic for helping me find my story. There is no way these books could have been written without their patience, support, and enthusiasm.

As Henri Matisse said, "Creativity takes courage." He was not joking!

Today, I want to thank you!

Thank you for your enthusiasm and questions and letters! They made writing these books a whole lot easier—and way sparklier! A book really isn't real or whole until it has been picked up and enjoyed, cover to cover. Thank you for sticking with Isabelle and Nora. Thank you for laughing at my jokes, for inviting me to your classrooms, for talking about the fairy godmother world (and the regular one, too). Thank you for sharing the sparkle!

When I was young, I was a lot like Isabelle. (Even now, I have a hard time reading the fine print!) I didn't like rules. But now I have to say: I sort of love them! They helped me write these books!

If you are interested in writing, here is my best advice: Get started! Keep a notebook. Draw. Explore. Take your time. Don't worry about being perfect. Instead, think big! Be bold! Take chances. Make lots of mistakes. To create these books, I had to write lots of words that were not good at all. I actually deleted two complete drafts! But thanks to family, friends, and my amazing editor, Anna Bloom, I found the stories. The process worked! Magic happened!

In book one, Isabelle needed kindness, determination, and gusto to become a great fairy godmother. The more I thought about these things, the more I realized how essential they are—no matter what we want to do.

We need to be kind—to others and ourselves. Especially when we are trying to do something big.

We need determination—to practice a lot—if we want to meet our goals.

And we need to have a whole lot of gusto and lots of exclamation points! When we care deeply about our stories, determination isn't so hard. Kindness comes easy. We smile more. We forgive ourselves. We enjoy the process! And when we can do all that, we can do anything! Happily ever after isn't just a line at the end of the story. It's real!

Sparkle on, readers.

Thank you so much for reading Isabelle's story.